LIFE ASSURED

Nicholas Rhea

This first world edition published in Great Britain 2007 by
SEVERN HOUSE PUBLISHERS LTD of
9–15 High Street, Sutton, Surrey SM1 1DF.
This first world edition published in the USA 2007 by
SEVERN HOUSE PUBLISHERS INC of
595 Madison Avenue, New York, N.Y. 10022.

British Library Cataloguing in Publication Data

Rhea, Nicholas, 1936-
    Life assured
    1.   Taylor, Matthew (Fictitious character) - Fiction
    2.   Insurance agents - England - Yorkshire - Fiction
    3.   Yorkshire (England) - Social life and customs - Fiction
    I.   Title
    823.9'14 [F]

    ISBN-13: 978-0-7278-6502-1

All Severn House titles are printed on acid-free paper.

Typese
Grange
Printed
MPG B

LIFE ASSURED

Previous titles in this series from Severn House

SOME ASSURED
REST ASSURED
SELF ASSURED

Dedicated to the memory of my parents

One

'LOST: Ginger cat, answers to Ginge.
Reward. Neutered. Like one of the family.'

From a parish magazine

With a broken leg in plaster following my motorcycle accident, I could not drive Betsy, my faithful little Austin 10 car. That meant I was unable to collect premiums from clients in my wild and beautiful moorland agency in Delverdale. They relied on me to visit them weekly or some-times monthly and inevitably had the right change ready. Almost everyone paid in cash. Some left it on window ledges or in outside toilets or even on farm gate posts and I knew that few liked to miss their regular payments. Missing a payment meant the money might be spent elsewhere, or be frittered away on something frivolous or unnecessary. In reality, that was highly unlikely because the moors people were anything but frivolous. Many regarded payment of their regular premiums as extremely important because they knew the insurance was designed to safeguard them during life's uncertainties. For many, it was the only way of saving and planning for the future and so they always wanted their policies to be up to date.

My immobility also meant I would be unable to canvas new clients or deal with renewals and claims – unless, of course, the clients came to my home.

I would find it very acceptable if they were prepared to do that, because I now had a larger house with an office and so they would not interrupt my domestic routine. For many clients, however, travelling to call on me was either impos-sible, very difficult or highly inconvenient, except for those within walking distance. Few had motor vehicles, even in the most remote parts of the moors and dales, and travelling miles through the hilly, winding lanes by horse or bicycle was far from easy. They therefore relied on the infrequent train service or even more infrequent bus. Travelling miles by public transport to pay a small insurance premium was neither sensible nor financially viable, to say nothing of the time spent hanging around for the return transport. In those moors, trains and buses did not come every few minutes – it was more like two trains a day and a bus once a week on market day.

All of this meant my broken leg was a major inconvenience. My inability to drive or visit my clients meant I was officially on the sick list, which in turn meant I received only a basic salary from my employers, the Premier Assurance Association, and the lack of new business meant I was not earning any commission. Commission was a vital supplement to my income, particularly as I had a wife and small son, but also because I had recently taken out a mortgage on a house and bought a car, with all the ongoing expenditure such possessions generated. Naturally, I was insured against an inability to work through sickness, injury or disease but the relevant policy did not begin to pay benefits until three months after I had been incapacitated.

Suffering only from a broken leg, I was otherwise quite fit and healthy and therefore unlikely to be off work for three months or more. The probable period would be eight weeks or thereabouts and so I could not rely on the Premier's sickness benefits to supplement my income. Evelyn, my wife, could earn small amounts through her supply teaching, but that was very spasmodic with sometimes only a day's work a month or even in an entire term; anything she earned was saved for special purchases or luxuries and we did not consider it part of our weekly income.

Then the indefatigable Evelyn had a bright idea. If I was compelled to stay at home, she reckoned I could look after our son Paul, do the housework as best I could, wash the clothes and do the dusting, cook the meals and generally function as a sort of house-husband. My pot leg would hamper me to some extent, but I was not completely immobile and could hop around the house and garden with the aid of a crutch. I could also complete my routine office work, write letters, answer the telephone, respond to callers at the door and generally ensure that my fledgling business remained active. Because Evelyn could drive Betsy, she was confident about undertaking all my routine tasks such as collecting regular premiums and delivering renewal application forms to clients; she might even drop off leaflets about new schemes and re-designed policies, giving people plenty of time to consider fresh investment opportunities before I returned to work. She might even canvas some new clients, and there were maturing policies to consider too, which often involved the pleasurable task of delivering a large cheque to the policyholder.

I explained that such cheques originated at Head Office and were posted to me for hand delivery, so that often only a receipt was required from the client. Quite often where policies had matured, people were keen to invest in another one, usually a type of life insurance. As I considered Evelyn's suggestion, I realized I had all the necessary records in my office and could guide her around the agency, advising her how to retrace my footsteps in the hamlets and villages day by day, and highlighting the risks, problems and personalities she might encounter.

I could warn her against the handful of bad payers and regular dodgers but the suggestion that she should deputize for me seemed sensible and, more importantly, it would help to maintain our income. It would also enable me to keep in fairly close touch with my clients whilst I was temporarily grounded at home. There was always the possibility that some clients might make alternative arrangements for their regular payments or, if they were in Micklesfield, find time to visit me if they had any special requirements or problems. I had telephoned the local shops and post offices in the villages within my agency to let them know of my circumstances because I knew it was from such places that village news was very efficiently broadcast. I couldn't ring all my clients – in fact, few of them had telephones and to write to everyone would be both time-consuming and expensive. Word of mouth was by far the most effective method of communication in such a sparsely populated area. In spite of my concern, I knew my current state of health would quickly become known – and that it would not last forever! It was nothing more than a temporary hiccup in my work.

As I had often talked to Evelyn about the quirkiness of some clients, I had no doubt she was perfectly capable of understanding and undertaking the task she had suggested. Her ability to communicate with people at all levels was never in doubt. She was most efficient as well as being a very likeable young woman, even though I say so myself. Furthermore, she was most trustworthy and considerate. Another bonus was that she was known to many of my clients due to her supply teaching at Graindale Bridge Roman Catholic primary school. It was attended by lots of pupils from within my agency. Another factor was that most of the people at home during the day were women, many being the mothers of small children and wives of men who worked away from home. Few men were at home during the day: anyone who was in the house was probably a shift-worker or an old-age pensioner. Or someone who was ill! As my working deputy, therefore, I felt Evelyn would be ideal. The big question was whether my bosses at District Office or even Head Office would allow this to happen. I was fully aware I could not allow Evelyn to go about my duties without the knowledge and approval of higher authority. I thought it would be interesting to obtain their views.

'Shall I ring Mr Wilkins, or will you?' Evelyn asked at breakfast one Tuesday morning. Mr Wilkins, the District Ordinary Branch Sales Manager: Life, was my immediate boss who operated from District Office in Ryethorpe. As he often accompanied me during my rounds, he knew Evelyn quite well and was also fairly familiar with my agency. He seemed the right person to approach and, if necessary, to put our proposal to Head Office.

'Hello, Mr Wilkins,' I greeted him, shouting down the

telephone as one tended to do. 'It's Matthew Taylor from the Delverdale agency.'

'Ah, Mr Taylor. How's the leg coming on?'

I provided an account of my rather slow progress, saying I was still sporting a heavy cast and clumping around the house like an elephant with a wooden leg, adding that otherwise I was very well. Then I provided a résumé of Evelyn's idea.

'It would please my clients if she went around and collected premiums,' I ventured to suggest, giving the reasons which were based on my local knowledge.

'Fine, collecting is not a problem for her, but what about the other aspects of your work?'

'If there was a renewal of any kind or even a maturity, I could brief her about the procedures and, if she could get the forms signed, I could do the administrative work at home. I have all the necessary records in my office and could look after the accounts, book-keeping, statistics, monthly returns, letter-writing and so on. I would keep a very close eye on what she was doing, day by day, and she is the sort of person who would always seek advice when it was needed. She would never take risks and I know she would be an asset to the company.'

He listened patiently as I outlined my version of the plan, particularly those benefits that would flow towards the Premier in the form of a continuation of regular income and repeat business in the form of renewals – perhaps even with some new business. I emphasized I would rather have Evelyn doing my rounds than some other relief agent nominated by Head Office – the moorland people rarely took kindly to strangers dealing with their personal matters.

I told him Evelyn could be very persuasive when necessary and reminded him that she had come up with this idea, which was good evidence of her desire to help. I also thought the status of the Premier would rise in the estimation of my clients: they would feel they were being looked after whilst their concerns were being addressed by the Premier's chief officers.

'You put forward a good argument, Mr Taylor, and in

my view, there is no problem,' he said when I had finished.
'Your wife is to be congratulated upon her initiative.
However, so far as Head Office is concerned, I do not need
to obtain their specific approval – there are many prece-
dents for this kind of situation, where family members and
even retired insurance agents have helped in such temporary circumstances. From our point of view, it means the
business continues, which in turn gives assurance to all our
clients. That is very important. Our clients are our most
important asset, as I am sure you appreciate, and their inter-
ests must take precedence over external factors.'

'I understand.'

'As your wife is to fulfil part of your duties, with you
continuing to supervise and advise her, I am allowed to
approve your proposal without recourse to Head Office,
although they must be made aware of the arrangements. I
will attend to that. So the short answer, Mr Taylor, is yes.
By all means thank your wife for her initiative and encourage
her to start immediately. There is no requirement to wait
for the formalities to be completed.'

'Thank you, that's a relief.'

'There is one point I should mention, however, Mr Taylor.
We cannot pay her a wage or expenses for the car and so
forth. We are already paying a salary to the Delverdale
agency through you. We will continue to pay that salary
and, of course, any expenses incurred. It will rest upon
you to make the necessary claims – telephone, postage,
car mileage and so forth. We will therefore continue to pay
your expenses even though you are officially on sick leave.
What we can do, however, is pay your wife commission
on any new business she generates and upon any repeat
business she deals with, such as renewals. It will be your
responsibility to make the necessary claims when you
submit your monthly returns. And we would appreciate a
letter from you as soon as you are able, outlining these
proposals, then our Regional Manager will respond with
a formal letter of approval which is the equivalent of a
contract. We need that for legal and procedural purposes
and, as I have told you, this kind of thing has been done

before, so your idea is not a problem. In fact, it will please Head Office.'

Evelyn became quite excited by the prospect and I spent most of that morning explaining how and where I collected premiums, showing her the entries in my collecting book which specified the date and amount due from each person. I listed each of the villages within my agency, noting upon which day I collected in each one. I explained to her that before she departed each morning, I would provide a reminder of where to find the premiums that would be left out when no-one was at home and if any policies were due for renewal, amendment or maturity, I would explain the procedures.

I assured her she would learn very quickly whilst reminding her to keep her eyes open for the dangerous antics of Crocky Morris, moorland sheep, dogs with no road sense, farmers on slow-moving agricultural vehicles and riders who still considered their horses superior to motor vehicles.

'So when shall I begin?' she asked.

'How about tomorrow?' I suggested. 'You can look through my records and books this afternoon with me explaining things, then tomorrow morning you could check the incoming post and deal with anything that arrives. I have to balance my books on Wednesday mornings, then bank my takings at the post office before one o'clock. As you know, Wednesday is also when I attend my market day 'surgery' outside the Unicorn. You could go there with me; I could hobble over there on my crutches, and you'd meet lots of clients and potential clients. And some fascinating market traders too, to say nothing of their customers!'

'Right,' she grinned. 'That's a good idea. And it just gives me time to drive into Guisborough to get myself a new costume for work. I've got to be smart if I'm deputizing for the man from the Premier.'

'So long as you don't try to claim it on expenses!'

And so began our new partnership.

Two

'Feeling depressed? Don't let worry kill you. Let the church help.'

From a parish magazine

I had set up my 'surgery' outside the Unicorn Inn at Micklesfield long before I had an office in my own house. I had done so because I realized it was important for me to be available at an established place and time if clients or potential clients wanted to make contact. With so few households having a telephone, communication could be difficult, particularly at short notice. It had seemed sensible, therefore, to make myself available at a place where people assembled on a regular basis – in this case Micklesfield village market. Even though I now had an office at home, however, my 'surgery' was continuing to prove most useful – people knew where to find me at least once a week and often combined a visit to market with a trip for a chat with me. Normally, of course, I would be away from the house during the working day, inevitably visiting one or other of the villages within my widespread agency, and sometimes being away from home until late in the evening. My work had no set hours and my schedule often meant visiting clients outside their own working hours. Those irregular absences often put me beyond the reach of many policy holders and potential clients, and consequently my 'surgery' was proving a great success.

Although Micklesfield was a typical moorland village with a small population, people from the whole of Delverdale came to the market every Wednesday by bus, train, car, horse or even pony and trap.

Most were women who were keen to purchase items unavailable in the local shops, although some men – especially pensioners – also came, chiefly because the Unicorn's bar was open all day. A lot of farmers and livestock traders came too, ostensibly to conduct business with their colleagues. There is little doubt that the atmosphere of the sturdy old inn with its stone walls, flagged floors, roaring log fires and ample space assisted greatly in helping to negotiate and conclude tricky deals. Lots of dealers' money changed hands in the Unicorn every Wednesday and on top of that the pub had an official market day extension of its hours. It was officially known as a general order of exemption, this kind of relaxation of opening hours being granted by the magistrates so that licensed premises could accommodate people attending public markets and so enable them to obtain essential refreshment. The pub opened in the morning at 10.30 a.m. and remained open all day until 10.30 p.m. with meals available if required. The inn's meals were very popular, and there was also a tea room for those who did not want to drink alcohol.

My needs were helped immensely because the pub was owned by Evelyn's parents, my in-laws, Derek and Virginia Mead. Derek was widely known as Big Deck, due to his size. It was he who had suggested I use the pub as a sort of office because it had a disused Bottle and Jug Department and, having recognized the potential, I agreed. He was supposed to be charging me a shilling rent each Wednesday, but would never accept money from me. However, I made sure I repaid him in other ways.

Fairly recent changes to the alcohol licensing laws had resulted in the Bottle and Jug sections of old inns becoming obsolete, but in their heyday, people and even children would arrive at the inn to buy ale, sometimes by the bottle but sometimes being poured from a jug into the customer's own container. Open containers of the kind sent by parents were rather a temptation to some children, hence the change in the law. Instead of entering the premises, they would make their purchases through a hole in the wall that opened directly on to the bar counter as a type of serving hatch.

In the Unicorn's case, that large hole remained with its thick glass window at the inner end and it had become a feature of interest which I hoped would never be blocked up or removed.

From my point of view the serving hatch – about a yard deep in the thickness of the wall and eighteen inches or so wide and high – was perfect for storing leaflets, books and other items, particularly if it was raining. I could stand near it to conduct my business, and in the worst weather could shelter either in the bar or beneath the covers of market stalls, knowing my papers were safe and dry. Another asset was that people could help themselves to brochures and leaflets and take them home to study; some were rather hesitant about approaching me in case I launched into some unwanted sales patter, although I never indulged in high-pressure salesmanship. Nonetheless, I marked every leaflet so that, if it came through the post to me after completion, I would know it had been collected from the Bottle and Jug.

In the short time I had been using this facility, I was pleased that completed application forms were being sent to me, some through the post and others being delivered by hand. In addition, I had found that many market customers and indeed some of the traders would approach me personally for help and advice.

Not surprisingly, my enterprise had become known as Matthew's Insurance and one of the stall holders, who made and sold house signs, had fashioned one for me as a gift when he discovered it was my birthday. It was now bolted on to the wall above the Bottle and Jug opening. It said simply: 'Matthew's Insurance'. Evelyn was familiar with the system because she would often help her mum and dad in the pub on market day, and so she was also known to most of the regular market traders – but not in the guise of an insurance agent! When she arrived with me that Wednesday, smartly dressed in her new, rather formal dark two-piece costume, she blushed at some of the wolf whistles. They came from anonymous places among the stalls but she tried to ignore them as she helped me stock the hole in the wall with my leaflets and papers. Inevitably, the stall holders were intrigued by her unexpected presence and several approached us for a chat, first asking about the progress of my leg and then quizzing Evelyn. It didn't take long for everyone to understand why she was not helping her parents that day. Similarly, customers of both the pub and market who were wandering among the stalls spotted her and went for a chat, ostensibly to ask after my progress but also to satisfy their own curiosity.

After half an hour or so, when I began to feel tired after standing and struggling with my crutches and heavy pot leg, she suggested I went into the bar to sit down. She was keen to spend time on her own, hoping to receive some enquiries and to chat with interested people on her own terms, and even to negotiate one or two policies. For Evelyn, this was effectively the beginning of her new role and it was obvious she was taking it very seriously. I felt she was enjoying it too and was confident she would cope.

When I hobbled into the bar, Big Deck insisted on buying me a pint of bitter and sitting beside me for a chat. I think he welcomed a brief break from his busy routine as he left the barmaid temporarily in charge. He was interested in the progress of my leg, how Evelyn and I were coping and whether or not we needed help. I assured him we were having no problems, other than those caused by the rigid and unrelenting weight of my leg which, by this stage, bore dozens of autographs scribbled by friends and family. Then he asked, 'Have you made contact with the new vicar?'

'Not yet,' I admitted. 'I knew we were getting one but didn't know he'd been installed, or whatever they do when a new vicar arrives.'

'Inducted, that's the word,' he said. 'Not that we go to his church, as you know, being Catholics, but he's a nice enough chap. Young and energetic, married with a couple of bairns and keen on motorbikes, so I'm told. He's called Salter. Jeremy Salter and he prefers to be addressed by his Christian name. He pops in here sometimes for a pint and a chat – not many vicars would do that, and he says he wants to meet you.'

'Meet me? Why does he want to meet me?'

'Dunno, he never said.'

'Maybe he wants something insuring. His bike, maybe? Or he might want his policies transferred to my agency – that's if he's with the Premier.'

'I reckon he'll have his own insurance system; it's called praying and asking God to look after him and his family.'

'God won't insure his motorbike or personal belongings, Deck! He'll need someone like the Premier to see to that.'

I couldn't think of any other reason why the new vicar would want to make contact, for although I had been brought up as a member of the Church of England, I wasn't a church-goer. I suppose I was a lapsed Anglican. If I did attend church, it was always with Evelyn. She was a Catholic and a regular member of the congregation at St Eulalia's Roman Catholic Church at Graindale Bridge. We'd been married there, Paul had been baptized there and, on special occasions such as Christmas and Easter Sunday, and on other occasions when I felt in need of the kind of peace offered by a church, I would accompany Evelyn to Mass. News that a Protestant clergyman wanted to make contact with me was therefore quite puzzling. I wondered if he had heard I was supporting the opposition. Perhaps he wanted to persuade me to correct the errors of my ways.

'He knows where you live,' Deck was saying. 'He didn't want to bother you when you were off work; he knows about you and your leg – through village gossip no doubt.'

'He could have popped in, I wouldn't have minded.'

'I told him that but then I said you normally came here on Wednesday afternoons, even with your gammy leg. He thought it was a great idea and said he would come here and see you, probably today.'

'So long as he doesn't want me to be a choir member or church warden! And I hope he doesn't start pressuring me to go to his services!'

'Just like you won't pressure him into taking out an insurance policy?' chuckled Deck.

Having dropped this puzzling matter into my proverbial lap, Deck returned to his bar duties, leaving me to wonder what the vicar wanted. I settled down to savour my pint as the trading, laughter and chatter continued around me. There were times I wondered where all these customers came from, and how they were able to take the necessary time away from their jobs or businesses. As I sat with my drink, several regulars paused to enquire about my progress and there was much good-natured banter about my condition, then Evelyn walked in, closely followed by a tall man wearing a clerical collar. He would be in his late thirties, I estimated, with a mop of rather long dark wavy hair and he wore a tweed jacket and cavalry twill trousers, albeit with a black shirt and the tell-tale clerical collar. He was taller than most of the other customers but as he moved through the crowded bar towards my chair, he was greeted warmly by many of them. Evidently he'd already made himself very well known in the Unicorn.

'This is Matthew,' Evelyn said as she halted at my table with him at her side, and I struggled to rise to my feet to greet the newcomer.

'No, don't get up,' said the vicar. 'Getting to your feet with that thing weighing on your leg must be like wearing a ball and chain. I'm Jeremy, the new vicar. Jeremy Salter. Everyone calls me Jeremy.'

He bent to shake my hand as I said, 'Nice to meet you, I'm Matthew Taylor. And you've evidently met my wife, Evelyn.'

'Pleased to meet you both. Now, do you mind if I join you?' he asked. 'I'd like a chat.'

'Please do.' I waved a hand to indicate the empty chair next to mine.

'Can I get you a drink?' was his next question before sitting down.

I accepted his offer. 'Just a half of bitter though; I've already got this one to finish!'

'And you, Evelyn?'

'No thanks, I'd better get back to my leaflets and customers!' And so she left us.

The Reverend Salter went to the bar, had a brief chat with Big Deck and returned to join me with a half of bitter in one hand and a pint in the other. He placed them on the table and settled at my side. I poured the half into my pint glass, raised it towards his pint and said, 'Cheers.'

He responded with his own 'cheers', then added, 'It's good of you to see me. I've heard about your accident but didn't like to bother you at home when you're supposed to be convalescing.'

'Deck said so, but I wouldn't have minded.'

'I heard about your insurance shop and thought it was a good idea to see you here. I enjoy coming to this little market; it's a wonderful reflection of village life, past and present.'

'My thoughts too, I enjoy it and it helps me do my job too.' I explained the reason for my presence, adding I'd missed a couple of weeks due to my injury.

'It's a fine way of meeting people on a regular basis,' he said. 'Like you, I'm often out of the vicarage on my rounds during the day and some evenings, and people find it diffi-cult to make contact. Maybe I should make a point of coming here each Wednesday – after all, we're both in a similar business, selling assurance of different kinds!'

We chattered about our respective work, with me explaining how Evelyn had volunteered to carry out some of my basic duties until I was fit, and he told me of his earlier parish in the Yorkshire Wolds. Then he got around to the real reason for his chat.

'When I first heard about your accident, I hesitated making contact but on reflection thought it might be just the thing to help your recovery. You'll have gathered this is not just a social visit, Matthew. I can call you Matthew?'

'Everyone does,' I said.

'It occurred to me that if you were at home all day with a broken leg, you might have time to spare with nothing to do, the perfect recipe for boredom!'

'Well, yes, the early days were rather hectic, mainly through trying to get accustomed to my pot leg and the crutches, but now I can cope and there's very little pain. I'm able to get about much more easily. Until I'm fully mobile, Evelyn is going to do my rounds and her sister,

Maureen, will look after our little boy whenever we need help. Paul's a playmate for Maureen's little lad, and it works very well. And with my leg on the mend, I was able to hobble over here today to show her my Bottle and Jug surgery! But I can't drive yet and so I'll be stuck at home for a few more weeks.'

'With not a lot to do with yourself?'

'I don't know about that! There's the housework, cooking, baby-minding, washing, not to mention my accounts and business records, so there's plenty to keep me occupied. I can manage most of that even with a pot leg, although it takes a long time.'

I could see my statement was not what he'd expected; I think he thought I would be sitting around all day with nothing to occupy me and that I would become bored very quickly – which is true. I would have become bored if there was nothing to occupy me but with Evelyn doing a large share of my work, I reckoned I could perform most of the household chores.

'Then perhaps I should not be so inconsiderate as to present you with my dilemma,' he said. 'It seems you have enough to keep you busy.'

'Oh.' I didn't know how to react. I had no idea what he wanted to ask. 'I thought you might be wanting to transfer your insurance?'

'No, I'm with an ecclesiastical insurance company – they specialize in vicarages and vicars, everything from life insurance to covering my motorbike. Sorry about that. I think we should forget my proposal, Matthew.' He did not explain further. 'Forgive me, I should have realized you were a busy man.'

'So what was it you wanted to put to me?' I was intrigued now and had no idea I had upset his plans, whatever they were.

He hesitated for a few moments, then said, 'You will know Mrs Henderson? A stalwart of the parish church?'

'Yes, I know her quite well.'

'Well, just after I arrived, I floated the idea of a parish magazine, something that would appeal to the villagers in general, and not just those who attend my church.'

'Well, yes, that's something we don't have in Micklesfield.'

'Exactly, and I think there's a need for one. You know the sort of thing – local news, gossip, adverts perhaps, church news, baptisms, weddings, funerals, topical stuff about Easter or Christmas . . . anything really. And Mrs Henderson – Ursula – said she would produce it. She knows a good local printer who will not charge the earth, and she's already been promised some adverts, which will help to pay for the printing, and has gathered enough material for the first issue.'

'I think it's a good idea!' I said. 'We could do with something that tells us what's happening in Micklesfield – advance news of events, a bit of local history and so on.'

'I'm pleased you think so, but the snag is that Ursula's sister has been taken ill and Ursula has gone down to Lincoln to look after her for an unspecified period. The long and short of it, Matthew, is that I need someone with local knowledge and the necessary skills to put the first issue of the magazine together, to edit it in other words, and oversee its production. Which is why I am here now, talking to you.'

'Me?' I was dumbfounded. 'But I don't go to your church, Jeremy. If I go at all, it's to the Catholic church in Graindale Bridge, with my wife and son. Apart from that, I've no church background, even if I am officially C of E.'

'I know that, but I'm sure you have the necessary skills. You must have; your job demands it. You have to compile accurate and legible claim reports about accidents, fires and damage, you need to present them clearly with a good command of English, and you need good business acumen too – how to make the best use of money. You could persuade people to place adverts! You know the village and its people, you get among them and talk to them. I know they all trust you, lots have told me so. I think you would be an ideal editor, but it might only be for the first issue. Ursula might return to continue where she left off. In short, that's what I was going to ask you.'

'But I've never done anything like this,' I began to protest. 'There's a huge difference between compiling official reports about insurance claims and editing a magazine.'

'It's all to do with the right use of words, Matthew, along with a bit of imagination and a flair for presentation. And, as I said, you might be needed to help with just the first issue. I should say we are hoping it will be a monthly magazine, and I am sure distribution will not be difficult. I have willing workers in my congregation who can deliver copies around Micklesfield, and we can leave them in the shop, post office, butcher's and garage for collection. It will be free, by the way, the idea being the adverts will pay for its production so you wouldn't have to worry about collecting subscriptions.'

'So when is it due, the first issue?'

'The end of next month. It's important we publish on time because some of the adverts, which have been paid for in advance, relate to events that have already been planned. That's really the problem – Ursula has done some of the work but I'll be honest and say a lot remains to be done.'

As we chatted, my brain was whirring at high speed, trying to gauge the demands that would be presented to me at home when Evelyn disappeared every day to collect my premiums from far-flung villages and hamlets. In addition to all the household chores and the garden, there was baby Paul to consider and, inevitably, there would be phone calls requiring my response and action. There was also the question of my ability – I had never considered myself good with words although I could compile a decent letter, and neither did I see myself as a magazine editor, even if it was nothing more than the local parish magazine. Nevertheless, I found the idea appealing.

'All right, Jeremy,' I said, seeing the expression of relief on his face. 'I'll have a go. So who is the printer?'

He named a small firm in Guisborough called Cockerels who had given an initial price based on eight octavo pages. They produced other parish magazines and a wide range of pamphlets, so were familiar with the traditional and well-tested layout and contents. Jeremy said the printers would need the raw material – the copy as he termed it – about ten days before publication date. Publication day had to be agreed in advance, and everyone had to work towards that deadline. He went on to say that Ursula had already collected a substantial amount of material, which she had left at the vicarage in a thick file, along with details of adverts already agreed. Jeremy said he wouldn't expect me to collect the file – he could bring it to my house and we agreed he should let me have it early the following day because there was no time to waste.

By way of celebration, he bought another round of drinks – a half pint each – and I began to wonder if I could stagger home with only one good leg. When the vicar had gone, I bought a couple of Virginia's rock buns and a pot of tea so I could provide Evelyn with some much-needed afternoon refreshment and went out to join her, with Virginia carrying the tray for me. As we stood by my depository of publicity material, I asked Evelyn how things were going.

'I've been very busy,' she said with a glow of satisfaction on her face. 'I've handed out lots of leaflets and a few proposal forms for endowment policies; they seem very popular with people who don't have a pension scheme at work. It's amazing how many husbands don't have a pension when they finish work. Two of the women who took proposal forms said they would bring them back next week, so I'm pleased about that. It shows they're really interested. Anyway, what did the vicar want?'

When I told her about his suggestion, she smiled. 'I think it's a good idea; the village needs something like that, especially if it's going to include everyone and not just church members. I think you'll do a good job, Matthew, even if it is for just one issue. I'll have words with Father O'Hagan at Graindale Bridge to see if he's got anything to include, and when I'm out on my rounds – your rounds, I should say – I can ask if there's anything anyone would like to include.'

'I think it's just for the Micklesfield people,' I pointed out. 'Not the whole of Delverdale.'

'Well, you can concentrate on Micklesfield first,' she said. 'If it's a success, and if it depends on adverts to pay its way, you might have to extend its catchment area to other villages. It's a nice challenge, Matthew, something to keep your mind busy while you're recuperating. I'm pleased you said you'd do it.'

As the market stall holders were preparing to dismantle their displays, we cleared our literature from the hole in the wall, carried it back to a small storage cupboard I was allowed to use in the Unicorn, then went to Maureen's to collect Paul before returning to our house. Tea would be a simple meal – gammon, sausage and eggs followed by a sherry trifle Evelyn had made earlier, and when Paul was put to bed we could relax.

But once Paul was in bed and asleep, Evelyn wanted to know all about the clients she would be visiting tomorrow. Instead of going through my books in the morning before setting off for Gaitingsby, she wanted to be fully prepared the night before.

And so I explained about Lord Gaitingsby's son who bred racehorses and whose insurance was due for renewal. Then there was the joiner, Wilf Burgess, whose cover for his workshop was also due for renewal. On my most recent visit, I had supplied both with renewal forms for completion and so they might be expecting me to call and collect them. It was important that such policies were renewed on the due date and not allowed to lapse. There were several other calls Evelyn would have to make for the collection of premiums, inevitably in small amounts of cash. I explained which households left their money out for the insurance man, which would pay by cheque (very few) and which might have no money and so offer something in lieu, like a sack of potatoes, a bag of apples, a dozen eggs or even a plucked chicken or duck. I told Evelyn it was her decision whether or not to accept such things in lieu of the monies due, with a reminder that if she did, it meant she would have to record the equivalent money in our accounts as payments received. In effect we were paying for those swaps and would have to make sure we put them to good use – or sold them on!

Next morning, after we had checked the post to find there was nothing to concern her, Evelyn set off in Betsy.

She now felt confident driving the little Austin 10 on her own and I had checked it for oil and water, tyre pressures and broken light bulbs. I also gave the brakes a short test and found everything in good working order. Evelyn looked very smart in her new outfit complete with briefcase containing my collecting book, various leaflets, plenty of small change and copying ink pencils. She had also packed a ham sandwich, a bar of chocolate and a flask of tea, plus an apple and an orange for her break time. I fussed a little too much, trying to remind her about the calls she would be expected to make, where to find the waiting money and who she should regard with a little caution or even suspicion. But she seemed confident and determined as I waved goodbye. I did not anticipate any problems.

Paul was to enjoy another day playing with his cousin Bernard – Maureen had said she would call and collect him when she went to the shop around ten o'clock. Jeremy the vicar rang to say he expected to be with me at half past ten, asking if that would be convenient, and I said it would be fine. I promised to have the kettle on when he arrived, and said I might even find a biscuit or two. And so the first day of my new era was beginning. The kettle had boiled before Jeremy Salter arrived and as we settled down to our cups of tea, he showed me Ursula Henderson's file. It turned out to be a shoebox full of scraps of paper with the words 'Parish Mag' on the lid. The contents were not filed in any kind of order but were nothing more than odds and ends, notes of ideas that had been thrown into the box.

'I'm sorry about this, Matthew, I didn't look in the box until this morning. Honestly, I thought she had started work but it seems she's done nothing with this lot.'

'I can see why she's suddenly rushed off to stay with her sister,' I said wryly as I ferreted among the contents. 'I don't think there's one complete item here. It's nothing more than bits of paper with ideas on them like "times of services", "history of the bell", "bats in the belfry", "village characters of the past" and so on. I wonder if she had any idea that all this had to be written up by someone? Perhaps she thought the printer would sort it out?'

'Oh dear, that's no good, no good at all. Look, I think I'd better call off the whole project, at least until there's more time to get it done properly. I can't impose this mess on you, not in its present state.'

'No, leave it,' I said. 'I regard this as a challenge and in some ways it's better if I start from scratch, rather than take over something half finished.'

'That makes sense.'

'Right, so if you can let me have your contribution – a nice foreword, times of your services, any special events during the coming months, baptisms, weddings and so forth, then I can see about filling the rest of the space. I'd need it as soon as possible. I can ring the garage, shop, post office, pub, undertaker, plumber and butcher, as well as Russell Hauliers and Bakers the builder to see if they will support us with an advert apiece, and they'll fill a page . . . The surgery will give us times of opening and their phone number, the parish council should be able to provide us with something about what they're doing right now, especially what's happening about that drain that gets blocked every time we have a decent shower of rain. PC Clifford might give us a bit of crime prevention advice and I know enough about the village history to fill another page. If you could provide a history of the church bell, we're in business.'

'Goodness, I'm breathless after that!' he grinned. 'Do you honestly think you can salvage something from all this?'

'There's only eight small pages to fill, Jeremy, but I wouldn't be surprised if there's enough material in this village to fill twelve. Even so, that's not much more than a decent school essay! I have a typewriter so I can produce something suitable for the printer, and I'm sure there will be bits and pieces in this box I can use. If any of our advertisers want to include drawings or logos, then they can be accommodated as well. I'm not sure whether we can reproduce photographs, like they do in newspapers.'

'Mr Cockerel told me photographs can be produced, and he'll make sure they are returned to their owners.'

'Great. I think the first thing for me to do is ring Mr Cockerel myself, to let him know what's going on, and also to find out precisely when he wants the copy and how he wants it, and whether twelve pages are a problem. Then I can have it ready on time.'

'I don't know what to say.'

'Whatever it is, say it when it's finished! Oh, and one other thing?'

'Yes?'

'We'll need a title. Is *Micklesfield Parish Magazine* sufficient, or do we give it a name?'

'I must admit I never thought of giving it a name. *Micklesfield Parish Magazine* sums it up, surely?'

'We could call it something like *Sanctuary*, followed by *The Parish Magazine for Micklesfield.*'

'I was rather hoping we could go beyond the church, to make it a magazine for the entire village,' said Jeremy. 'Its name should reflect that.'

'Then how about the *Micklesfield Magazine*? Simple but effective.'

'Yes, yes, I like that, Matthew. Use that one.'

'Do you need to get the permission of your parochial church council?'

'Not if it's a magazine for the entire village.' He smiled rather slyly. 'Parochial church councils tend to disagree a lot among themselves; they cause more problems than they solve, and there's a lot of people who like to exercise power which can sometimes be misplaced. Let's say it would be much easier if it was a magazine that was *not* church based, with the important decisions left to an editor, not a committee or council.'

'Ah, I understand.'

'I might say that the fact you are editing the first edition does distance it from the parish church, Matthew. I welcome that.'

'I can see you will be very popular with the village, Jeremy.'

'But not perhaps with the parochial church council!' he smiled. 'But I believe God operates beyond the walls of our churches. He works out there, in the countryside around us, in the villages, in the houses and schools, and always among the people.'

'I couldn't agree more.' I meant every word.

We chatted for a few more minutes over our tea and biscuits, with me informing him of the personalities and characters in Micklesfield and other parts of Delverdale, and then he left to visit a sick parishioner. I promised to keep in touch.

Now I had a project that would provide me with entertainment and occupation as my broken leg slowly healed.

Three

'A nearly full church had a minute's silence with a trumpeter from the village orchestra.'
From a parish magazine

With nothing in the morning post to demand my attention, and with Evelyn collecting premiums in the Gaitingsby area, I decided to begin work immediately on the magazine. I felt I could achieve a good deal before dinner time. Ursula Henderson's shoebox, with its untidy mass of notes and scribbled ideas, was the obvious starting point, even if I discarded much of the contents. I carried it into the kitchen and tipped everything on to the table, hoping to sort the mess into some kind of logical order.

Within half an hour or so, I had assembled several small piles of associated subjects. There were small advertisements from people wanting to sell second-hand items like bicycles, sewing machines and furniture, or even small animals such as puppies, kittens, chickens, ducklings and baby pet rabbits. She had secured promises for some larger advertisements from local businesses like the garage, builder, plumber and shop along with suggestions for topics such as the history of the village, the church and the Wednesday market. However, there was no indication of who was to write up those histories. Ursula had included a reminder about obtaining lists of the times of church services, surgery opening times, parish council activities, WI meetings and so forth, and then I found a scribbled piece of paper saying, 'Get Harry Wheeler to do a piece about his memories of Micklesfield.'

I knew Harry quite well. A familiar figure around the

area, he was reputed to be the oldest man in the village and had lived in Micklesfield for the whole of his life, always in the same house. He had been born at Lingfield House, lived there both as a child and youth, and had continued to occupy it as a married man with a family. He had earned his living as a farm contractor, beginning as a labourer and then hiring himself to farmers as a daytal man, on a daily basis, with the ability to perform any task on a busy farm. Later, with lots of the younger men being called up during both world wars, and with Harry then being too old for active service, he had recognized an opportunity to continue to make himself available to anyone willing to pay for his services, but in a different way. For that reason, he had worked even into his eighties, having acquired a plough, various horse-drawn implements such as a fertilizer drill, hay rake, reaper and swathe turner, as well as other machines, a cart and couple of horses. People said he had visited farm sales and friends to examine old and discarded implements and then, because he had not been able to afford expensive machinery, he had actually scrounged the necessary spare bits and pieces, and then built his own farm implements. He would offer his services along with the use of such equipment and it seems he had been very successful because he was comfortably off in his old age, and never short of cash. Like so many country people, he could always find ways of making a few shillings when necessary.

I was uncertain about his actual age, like everyone else in Micklesfield, probably because he was never quite sure himself, but, according to local knowledge, it was reasonably certain that he was in his nineties. Because of the memories he could produce during conversations, speaking of things he could vividly recall such as Queen Victoria's golden jubilee in 1887, the people who knew him well reckoned he was either ninety-two or ninety-three. He was now living alone because his wife, Ruth, had died several years ago, in her mid-eighties. With more than a little help from willing neighbours, he continued to live alone, being assisted with things like his weekly washing, Sunday dinner and general cleaning.

Harry was surprisingly fit, being able to walk to the shop and to make his daily trip to the pub for a couple of strong ales, albeit with the aid of a pair of sticks. He was instantly recognizable due to his slightly stooped appearance, big brown boots and the brown woolly hat that never seemed to leave his head, even indoors. He had a permanent growth of grey whiskers around his chin and cheeks, although this fertile area never seemed to mature into a full-blown beard. His two sons and one daughter all lived and worked some distance from Micklesfield, but one or other of them came to visit him most weekends to either take him out for Sunday dinner or to make it for him at home. According to Ursula's note, she felt Harry might write something about his memories of Micklesfield in former times, particularly as he had experienced such a long and busy life, always in and around the village with occasional excursions into other parts of the dale.

There was nothing in her notes to suggest she had put this idea to him, but his story-telling abilities were well known, especially when he was in the pub, and so I decided to telephone him. His family had insisted on him having a phone installed so that they could keep in touch from a distance. I looked up his number and asked the operator to obtain Micklesfield 16 for me.

''Ello,' shouted a voice after it had rung a few times.

'Is that Harry Wheeler?'

'Eh?'

'Is that Harry Wheeler?' I shouted back.

'You'll have to shout up, I'm a bit 'ard of 'earing.'

'Is that Harry?'

'Who else would it be? This is my phone you're ringing on.'

'It's Matthew Taylor, the insurance man,' I bellowed back.

'No, he's not 'ere, this is 'Arry Wheeler. 'E's got a different number 'cos 'e doesn't live 'ere.'

'I know, I'm Matthew Taylor . . .'

'You'll 'ave to ring 'im on 'is own telephone, I can't fetch 'im to this 'un, 'e lives down t'village.'

'No, look, Harry, I'm Matthew Taylor,' I shouted as loud as I could.

'Then why didn't you say so? Do you want to sell me some of your insurance? Not life insurance, not at my age. No thank you, Mr Taylor, I'm a bit past it now, never ailed a thing so why would I want insurance?'

I was sure he would replace the phone and cut me off before I had had a chance to make him understand the reason for my call and so I shouted as loudly as possible, 'I'm compiling the parish magazine . . .'

'Eh?'

'I said I'm compiling the parish magazine . . .'

'Do I want some margarine? Why would I want margarine? No thank you, I allus use best butter.'

'No, the parish magazine!'

'Perished margarine? Why would I want perished margarine? I wouldn't give that to my pigs.'

'I think I'd better come and see you,' I shouted as loud as I was able. 'It's about a piece for the parish magazine.'

'It's no good coming to here if you just want to sell me a piece of perished margarine, I allus use butter, like I said, Mr Taylor. Besides, I thought you were t'insurance man? Have you gone into selling margarine? I'd 'ave thought you'd be best sticking to t'insurance; margarine's not a patch on butter. Is it summat to do with you once working for t'butcher?'

I could see I was going to get absolutely nowhere with this conversation and although I wanted to achieve something positive with the production of the magazine, I still thought a contribution from Harry would be worth a little effort on my part. I felt sure the magazine needed something personal and interesting instead of being little more than a list of times and events.

In addition, of course, I had walked, or hobbled, my way to market outside the Unicorn yesterday and so I knew I could reach Harry's house without too much trouble, even if it meant climbing a very steep incline with my pot leg and the aid of a crutch. If I could talk to him for only ten minutes, I might be able to convince him of my real requirements.

'I'll come and see you,' I shouted into the telephone.

'Well, do as you like, but don't expect me to buy any o' that margarine.' And with that he slammed down his receiver.

Wasting no more time, I found a small notebook and pencil in case I had to write down my requirements and left home on my mission. Although it meant a tough climb for about half a mile, I found myself coping even if the effort made me pant heavily. After about ten minutes, I reached Harry's house in its splendid setting on the hillside. Although it bore the name Lingfield House which might imply it was a large establishment, it was really nothing more than a stone cottage which had been built by his grandfather. Its strength was its stunning location with views across the dale; townspeople and visitors would yearn for such a house, but for Harry the views meant little. All he required was a solid stone house which would keep out the weather, yet be cool in summer and warm in winter without costing a fortune to heat. I knocked on the back door, realizing he was unlikely to hear me, then opened it and shouted.

'Harry? It's Matthew Taylor.'

I walked straight in as I did with many of the clients within my agency. The back doors of peoples' homes were rarely if ever locked, even during the night hours although front doors were kept locked and closed, simply because no-one ever used them for ordinary visits. Front doors were used only for the deceased to be carried out for a funeral, or for a bride to leave on her way to a wedding and perhaps for a very important visitor who would be offered tea in the best room, often accompanied by the smell of rising damp and mothballs. Inside, I shouted again and rapped on the door that I knew led into his parlour. I'd been into his house on several occasions and knew he would be sitting there, probably with a cat on his knee in front of the fireplace.

'Harry?' I shouted as loud as I could.

'Come in, t'door's open,' he shouted.

'Now then, Harry,' I greeted him when I went in. 'Don't get up . . .'

He was sitting just as I had expected, as he could usually be found with his favourite cat on his knee, and I went to the other side of the fireplace and settled in an easy chair. That's how things were done in these parts.

'I hope you're not wanting to sell me some o' that rotten margarine,' he grunted. 'And if it's insurance you're wanting to sell, that'll be a waste o' time an' all. Why would I want insurance at my age? I've enough put by to see me sided away when t'time comes. Even if I hadn't a bit put by, they'd never leave me to top, would they? Somebody would see to me.'

'I'm not selling margarine and I'm not trying to persuade you to take out any insurance, Harry.' I used a loud voice but talking to him face to face was easier than using the telephone. He could hear me quite clearly if I kept my voice raised and faced him squarely. 'I've been asked to produce a village magazine, the *Micklesfield Magazine*.'

'Magazine? Not margarine?' He chuckled at the news.

'Right. A parish magazine – well, not really a parish magazine. It's going to be for the whole village, with articles about the place and the people. I was wondering if you'd like to write something, maybe one of your stories about old times.'

'Me? Put pen to paper, for other folks to read? Folks who've learned things from books?'

'Yes, I know you can do it, you can tell a very good story.'

'Telling a tale's one thing, Matthew, but writing it down's another. I never went to school, you know, I know nowt about spelling or punctuation and such, and even letters get jumbled when I try to read.'

'But you read a lot; I've seen you looking at magazines and newspapers, and even books sometimes.'

'Looking at pictures, Matthew. Allus looking at pictures. Seeing how machinery's made, working out how folks manage to put things together, bit by bit, how they make machines work and do jobs for us. Like motor cars. Clever stuff, that, much cleverer than learning from books. Not that I've ever tried to build myself a motor car.'

'Somebody said you made your own machinery? When you hired yourself out on a daytal basis?'

'Aye, I did. I couldn't afford to buy expensive things so I made my own. I got the bits at sales and so on, never paid for anything though. I would offer half a day's work to get my hands on an old plough which I could use for spares. Or any old bits of useful metal and wood. That sort of thing, trading my skills for goods and pieces I could use. I've built a few carts in my time, I can tell you. And other things.'

'Bartering?' I smiled. 'I do a bit of that myself. If a client can't pay, I'll take something in lieu, like a dozen eggs or a side of ham, or whatever.'

'It's a good system, Matthew. You can get by without money but you can't get by without food and clothes and somewhere to sleep. You can allus do a deal for that sort o' thing. Swap one thing for another.'

'So could you write me a piece about that? How you built your own plough or hay rake? Or anything you made out of spares and old pieces.'

'Nay, lad, but I could draw a picture for you, with measurements. A plan. I can draw quite well but I'm no good with words.'

'Could you?'

'Aye, I've got some sketches. I kept 'em in case I 'ad to use 'em again. I'll show you. Just you sit tight there while I look in yon chest o' drawers.'

As he moved, the cat leapt from his lap. Harry ferreted in a deep drawer, one of a chest in a corner of the parlour. He pulled out a deep file of papers, worn and browned around the edges because they were not kept in any kind of box or wallet. He took one from the top and handed it to me. It was the drawing of a plough, the kind used for digging in light soils, but the sketch had been exploded so that constituent parts could all be seen in relation to one another. There were measurements too, with details of the length of the shafts, diameter of the wheel and angle of the blade.

'I drew that,' he said with evident pride. 'Then went

around looking for the bits I needed and made it for myself. Some ploughs have higher handles than others, for taller blokes, but this 'un was made to measure for me. Good ploughs were made to fit their handlers and their horses, and built for the locality, that's why good plough makers were hard to find.'

'So you made your own?'

'Aye.'

'Did you make them for anyone else?'

'Nay, lad, there was no time. I was far too busy earning a living to bother with making ploughs and things for other folks.'

'Would you mind if I reproduced this drawing in the magazine? Along with a few words, which I'll write up from what you've told me. I'll bring the article here and read it over to you, before it is printed, just to make sure it's all correct and that you agree with it all.'

'Can you make a picture of my plan? For a magazine?'

'The printer will be able to do that; it won't damage your sketch and I'll make sure you get it back.'

'Well, Matthew, I never thought my efforts would ever see the light of day in a magazine! So yes, you can take that one with you and write up something. Mebbe if folks like it, we might do another?'

'That's what I'm hoping to do, Harry. If the villagers like the magazine we'll print it every month, and it's always nice to have items from village people. Memories of the past are always popular. I think this will be a wonderful start, something so very original like this plan; it's far better then reading lists of opening times for the surgery, or the times of church services!'

And so it was that I made my first 'scoop', as I thought of it. I was convinced that very few people would know about Harry's plan-drawing skills, or his ability to create his own machinery and equipment from scrap pieces. As I left him looking through his pile of other drawings, I wondered where his first plough was now. Was it still in the village? In the excitement of making this discovery, I had omitted to ask what had happened to his plough but thought the article, when it was published, might generate some interest. It might even help to locate it.

My chat with Harry meant I had something interesting to tell Evelyn when she got home, but now I must return to my chores, make myself a light dinner and decide how to tackle the remainder of the *Micklesfield Magazine.*

But even before reaching home, I had an idea. It arose as I mulled over my visit to Harry. We were going to call it the *Micklesfield Magazine*, and by making full use of that alliteration, I could name the contents so that each major part began with the letter M. Harry's piece, and anything that followed, would be Micklesfield Memories. Maybe Danny Randall at the garage would provide a piece about Motoring around Micklesfield with advice on car maintenance and road safety. We could print the Month in Micklesfield with dates of forthcoming events, and perhaps I could persuade an accountant or bank manager to write a piece offering financial advice: Money in Micklesfield. There could be news from Micklesfield Market, Mornings in Micklesfield, Micklesfield Moments (a light-hearted column) and the Micklesfield Miscellany, a collection of unconnected but interesting bits and pieces. I thought of Mirror on Micklesfield, Manufactured in Micklesfield, and many more. By the time I returned home my mind was buzzing with ideas and I couldn't wait to see what else lay among Ursula's papers. Already I was wondering about the 'shape' of the magazine. If I put Harry's plan of a plough on page three, with page one containing the introduction and contents, and page two showing the times of church services and other events under the heading of the Month in Micklesfield, how was I going to use the rest of the space to provide the necessary balance and style for our new magazine?

As I walked into the house, however, I was brought back to normality because the telephone was ringing.

It was a client from Baysthorpe who wanted to amend his insurance policy because he had just changed his car. I could easily deal with that matter on the phone and promised to send him the necessary form to complete and sign.

In the meantime, I issued him with a cover note bearing his new car number until the formalities had been concluded. Next I rang the printers at Guisborough, to seek further advice on presentation and pagination, and Mr Cockerel was most helpful.

My midday meal, called dinner in the moors, was next on the agenda, and quite suddenly I realized that time was whizzing past and that I must find something for that night's cooked tea. The afternoon promised to be equally time-consuming and Evelyn would expect me to prepare something to come home to after her first day collecting on my behalf. I knew I could not make the excuse that I had been too busy! For my dinner I made a poached egg on toast which I ate while ploughing through Ursula's papers, making yet another sift of her suggestions and putting to one side those items I felt would be suitable for the first edition of the *Micklesfield Magazine*. By mid-afternoon I could visualize the appearance and content; now I must type some of the items and work out precisely how the pages would appear. Following my chat with Mr Cockerel I knew the pages could only be in multiples of four and our first magazine looked as though it would require more than eight, judging by the amount of material on my desk and spread across the kitchen table.

To help me plan the layout, I selected three sheets of foolscap paper from my desk, folded them in half and placed them together, like a blank magazine of twelve pages. I numbered them, sketched the cover, roughed in the adverts and suddenly saw the magazine taking shape as I worked.

Then the telephone rang. I answered with, 'Matthew Taylor, Micklesfield.'

'Is that the insurance man? Matthew's insurance?' It was the voice of a well-spoken woman whom I did not recognize.

'Yes, can I help you?'

'I need to discuss a delicate matter of insurance with you, Mr Taylor. Maybe you could call for a chat?'

'Well, I'm off work at the moment with a broken leg

and so I can't drive out to my clients. I'll be out of action for a few more weeks, but you are welcome to come here if you are ever in Micklesfield. I can deal with a lot of work at home.'

'Oh, I see. Well, I live in Micklesfield and it is rather urgent, so I will call in. How do I find you?'

I provided directions to my house, giving her the route to the office door, and she then surprised me by saying she would arrive in ten minutes. I asked for her name and she said, 'Laura de Genièvre,' followed by a pause as if she expected me to recognize the name. I didn't, although on the phone she did sound very upper class – even haughty.

I wondered whether I should clear away the debris from Ursula's box, for it was littering the kitchen table, but decided against it, especially as I had directed the lady to my office door. There was no reason why she should come through the house or kitchen and so I thought I did not need to tidy the place. However, I did hurry into my office to tidy and dust my desk so that I might present an air of efficiency. The moment I had completed a very brief and flustered cleaning session, there was a knock on the back door. I wondered who it might be, for I had directed Laura de Genièvre to my office via the route which used the front entrance. I hurried to respond and, outside the back door, I found a very elegant and smartly dressed lady. Her clothing was definitely not of the kind one associates with village life on the North York Moors; it was more in keeping with the social scene in a major city like London or Paris. In admiring her dress sense, I found it difficult to estimate her age but she looked in her mid-fifties, very slender and of medium height. She had light brown hair in a short, neat style and a long, narrow face with blue eyes and good teeth.

'Good afternoon, Mr Taylor,' she smiled. 'Laura de Genièvre. I am sorry to arrive at such short notice and it is good of you to see me, especially in your condition.' And she smiled as she noticed my leg with its casing of plaster. Despite her name, however, there was no trace of a French accent when she spoke.

'Come in.' I held open the door and stepped back to admit her. 'Excuse the mess in the kitchen; I'm working on a magazine. But come through to my office.'

'Yes, you said I should go to your office but I am told that everyone uses the back door in this village, and I do want to settle in as quickly as I can. I am so keen to adapt to your local customs and practices.'

I led her through the house, my pot leg being cumbersome as I negotiated doorways and furniture, then I was able to settle her on a chair before my desk as I went round to take my usual seat. I felt like an employer conducting the interview of a potential employee, but immediately I could see she was interested in the view across the dale. The front windows of our house enjoyed spectacular long-distance views which, at times, we might take for granted. Such long distance views were commonplace for the local people, but newcomers found them enchanting.

'Can I get you a drink?' I offered.

'No thank you, Mr Taylor. I do not intend staying long, and I do not wish to keep you from your work. I wish only to explore the possibility of taking out an insurance policy with you – I might add, my insurance cover has always been in London, where I was based until my retirement, but now that I am living here, I wish to make use of local business people and tradesmen where possible. And as my present insurance has just expired, you will understand why I am here.'

'Expired?' I was worried about that word. I always ensured that my clients' policies were renewed well ahead of their expiry date, so that cover was continuous. I was fully aware that many people made claims only to discover they had not renewed their policies, and consequently such claims could not be met.

'Yes, that is why I have come at rather short notice. I need to renew my insurance and thought it was an opportunity to switch to a local company. Yours. I believe you call yourself Matthew's Insurance?'

'That's the name I've been given by the local people, but actually I am employed by the Premier Assurance

Association, one of the country's largest insurance companies.'

'Ah, that is good. I know of the Premier. Now, Mr Taylor, I am recently retired and have just come to live in Micklesfield, and it was during the upheaval of moving house that I omitted to renew my policy.'

'Then we need to act quickly,' I said. 'So what sort of insurance cover do you require?'

'My legs,' she said.

'Your legs?' I frowned.

'Yes, they are very important to me. I have looked after them well during the years, and they have earned a good living for me.'

I did not know how to respond. Everyone had legs but not many people bothered to specially insure them; not even my legs had been insured and I was now living proof that things could go wrong with them!

She was alert enough to notice my hesitation and for a second time I wondered if I should recognize her name.

'I was a ballet dancer, Mr Taylor. My legs were vital to my art; without them I could not continue and if I had damaged them, I could not have earned my living or fulfilled my contracts.'

'Ah, now I understand. Yes, I can see how important it would be.'

'Precisely, so throughout my career I had them insured – very well insured, I might add. Understandably, conditions were imposed. I could not go roller-skating or ice-skating, for example, and I was not allowed to go fell walking, rock-climbing or skiing, nor could I partake in other dangerous sports or pastimes such as repairing my roof. Not that I ever wanted to!'

'I think the Premier would impose similar conditions now.'

'I would expect that, Mr Taylor. Now I will explain my plans. Even though I retired some time ago, I continued to dance, partly to keep myself fit but also as a part-time teacher. But that was very low key; it was in North London where I used to live. It is that kind of activity I wish to start here, in the village hall. I want to organize ballet classes, mainly for children, although I wouldn't reject interested adults. That means my career now differs from the original when I was an artiste making stage appearances around the world, but my legs will still be vital as I will have to demonstrate the various sequences and steps. In addition, I am told by the secretary of the hall that I must have adequate insurance if I am to be responsible for children and others on the premises.'

'Yes, that's standard practice.'

'I must add that plans are very fluid at the moment. It is little more than an idea, but I need to investigate the feasibility of it all, along with any rules and regulations, before I commit myself.'

'I'm sure you realize the hall has its own public liability insurance, but all outside agencies making use of the premises are advised to provide their own individual cover to cater for their particular needs.'

'I understand, Mr Taylor. So there are two parts to this. First, I need to re-instate the insurance to cover my precious legs, which are about to earn their living in a different way; and second, I need to explore the right kind of cover required if I am to conduct ballet dancing classes.'

'I think we should insure your legs and we must do so immediately. Perhaps incorporated into a life and injury policy? I am sure we can cover you but have no idea how much the premiums will be; that is a matter for the Premier to decide, so I will ring my District Office before you leave. With their approval, we can complete a proposal form and get it in the post tonight; you'll then be covered from today. That will take care of your legs! I think we should wait until your plans for the classes are clearer.'

'Yes, but I thought we could negotiate the necessary insurances at the same time.'

'Not really. The insurance for your legs is a purely personal matter, one which requires insurance cover wherever you are, both in the hall and outside, wherever risks lie. I can deal with that immediately.'

'Good, then we shall go ahead.'

'Your second insurance is quite distinct and separate, and rather more complex. You'll need a business and public liability insurance to cover the children in your care, but must wait until your plans are more concrete. The Premier will want precise details of your plans, the venue, the number of people and children expected to be present, the frequency of classes, details of other people involved such as a pianist or assistant, and a host of other matters. There is no problem with this; it's just a question of knowing all the relevant facts. We need those before we can issue the necessary policy.'

'Oh, I see. That's quite clear now. I'll obtain more details and let you have them before I open for business.'

'Good. Now, the insurance of your legs. I must ring my District Office just to check we can go ahead with this kind of rather specialized policy.'

With Miss de Genièvre at my side, I rang my District Office at Ryethorpe and asked to speak to the District Sales Manager, John English. After explaining the type of insurance required, he asked about my client. I provided her name whereupon he said, 'Ah, yes, the ballerina. She was in the news some time ago, she got her legs insured for a huge amount – half a million pounds, if my memory serves me correctly. But if she's no longer performing on the world stage, then I am sure she will not require such a large amount of cover. It is well established that everyone has an unlimited insurance interest in his or her own life, Mr Taylor so, yes, we can accept her. We do similar policies for professional footballers, pianists and magicians – in the latter cases it's the fingers that are insured. It is just a question of determining the amount in association with the risks involved, and calculating the premium. Get her to fill in a proposal form with the amount of cover required; we can incorporate it with a life policy if she wishes, then we will contact her when our actuaries have calculated the premium. The other cover, for the ballet classes, is not a problem either. She is wise to take out adequate cover just in case she gets herself involved in any kind of civil claim if a child is injured whilst in her care. Let us know when she wants us to go ahead with that one. So, well done, Mr Taylor, a couple of interesting new policies in the pipeline.'

Miss de Genièvre was delighted and I was able to present her with a proposal form to cater for her immediate needs; it was a simple adaptation of a proposal form for a life insurance combined with a personal injury policy. I told her that the Premier would contact her in due course, through me, and reminded her to keep me informed about progress with her plans for ballet classes. I asked her to consider the house insurance too, and any other things of value she owned.

'My house isn't insured, Mr Taylor. I've always rented flats; I've always been on the move, you see . . .'

I explained the benefits, and she said she would think about it all.

'Thank you,' she said, getting ready to leave. 'I am most grateful for your response, Mr Taylor, in spite of your own leg problems! And thanks for reminding me about my house insurance! I am sure I will go ahead with that, but in the meantime will try to gauge the sort of response I might get to the ballet classes idea, and I'll get in touch when I have more news.'

'Why don't I include a piece in our new magazine?' I suggested. 'This is the very first issue.' I told her how I had become involved with the proposal. She listened and smiled.

'I came here to be anonymous, Mr Taylor, to retire from audiences and fans and publicity, but already I am finding life very boring, hence my wish to start a ballet class. It would be nice if the children knew a little about me and my previous successes, so yes, I'll be pleased to help with your magazine.'

'I need to fill only half a page,' I said. 'So I don't need many words. Can you produce something for me? Something to whet the appetite of your potential dancers? A couple of hundred words, perhaps, and even a photo if you have one. Perhaps of you on stage somewhere?'

'That will be my pleasure, Mr Taylor.'

And so that was another half page filled!

Now, with quite a lot of excitements to tell Evelyn, it was time to prepare her tea.

Four

'Village Hall Extension. Official Opening 27th April. Please note that the village hall will be closed until the opening. It will be closed again after being opened, but will be open temporarily on the 24th for a rehearsal of the opening after which it will be closed until the opening. It will remain closed for a while after the opening after which opening times and closing times will be as normal.'

From a parish magazine

E velyn was thoroughly enjoying her visits to the villages scattered around Delverdale and came home each evening with tales of her exploits as she collected premiums from my clients. As she executed this vital work on my behalf, I dealt with a range of insurance matters which presented themselves at our house, either in the form of letters through the post, personal callers or telephone calls. Also requiring my immediate attention was a good deal of official correspondence from District Office, a large amount of which was to remind clients of renewal dates or changes to some of the benefits contained in endowment policies.

In between times, I worked hard to solicit and prepare material for the first draft of Micklesfield's new magazine. It was more difficult than I had anticipated, chiefly because many of the contributors had no appreciation of how important it was to make sure their written work was spelled correctly or the facts contained within their submissions were accurate. I was rather dismayed at how many failed to read over and check their work to see if it contained errors.

Another task was to identify and eliminate those funny phrases that seem to appear in so many amateur publications, particularly parish magazines. It was my job as editor to recognize such *faux pas* before the material went to press, although I must admit I considered retaining a few of the kind that appear on the headings of these chapters. They would generate a good deal of unconscious but welcome humour. Quite often, the funny pieces resulted from carelessness on the typewriter so far as checking one's spelling or being careful as far as the meaning of words was concerned. This kind of problem could be eliminated simply by reading over one's work. There were many more examples, the first from an advertisement which read, *Excelsior Café. Fish and Chips: 3s.0d. Sausage and Chips: 2s.6d. Old Age Pensioners: 1s.6d.* Another came from instructions on a tinned pudding: *This pudding should be cooked slowly in a moderate oven and will have the same taste and texture as your grandmothers.* I loved the obituary about a local man which read, *He was an enthusiastic and talented amateur photographer. He specialized in pictorial photographs and was especially fascinated by scenes which included lakes, rivers, streams, ponds and waterfalls. Indeed, he could never pass water without taking a pictorial record of it.*

Perhaps one of the worst errors was in the Deaths column of a local newspaper. It read, *In loving memory of John William Brown who pissed away peacefully in hospital.*

Within a week of agreeing to compile the magazine, I had compiled my planned presentation for the first draft and calculated the pagination along with the layout of each of the twelve pages, particularly those containing important advertisements or current announcements.

As I battled with this voluntary work, my leg was improving and growing stronger almost by the day. There were still several weeks before I would have the heavy plaster removed and thus be able to move with welcome ease. Then around eleven o'clock one morning, when Evelyn was collecting in the higher reaches of Delverdale, I was about to break for a cup of tea and a scone. The kettle was already singing and the teapot was on the draining board, awaiting the hot water. Then someone knocked on the back door. As local people tended to come to the back door rather than the front, I assumed it was a villager or a client. Paul was once again being cared for by his Aunt Maureen and so I had the house to myself with magazine contributions strewn all over the kitchen table. Ignoring my crutch, I made good use of the table and back of the chairs for support as I hobbled to answer the door. When I opened it, I found a tall, slender and very attractive young woman standing there. She was a complete stranger, smartly dressed in a bottle-green costume with a white blouse and black shoes. I'd estimate her age at about thirty-five; she had dark wavy hair worn quite long and a warm, friendly face with a ready smile. I had no idea who she was.

'Mr Taylor?' she asked as I hopped into the doorway.

'Yes, Matthew Taylor. Sorry about this . . .'

'Don't worry, I've heard about your accident and didn't know whether I should disturb you.' Her accent was most certainly not from any part of Yorkshire. I detected a southern trace in her speech – the Home Counties, I'd guess. 'I hope you don't mind me calling without an appointment?'

'Not at all, it happens all the time. Come in.' I stepped back to allow her to enter the house. 'Sorry about the mess on the kitchen table, I'm compiling a village magazine.'

'Yes, I heard about that too. It's good of you to offer your services like this.'

'It's keeping me occupied. So is it something to do with insurance?'

'Yes, I suppose so, and the magazine.'

'Ah, well, follow me through to the office, it's tidier! I was about to make myself a pot of tea; the kettle is boiled and two cups are as easy to make as one.'

'That's very kind of you. I hope I'm not intruding.'

'Not at all, it's nice to have company. Now, there'll be a cup in this cupboard and milk in the pantry . . . do you take sugar?'

'No, just milk.'

And so I found a tray, made a pot of tea, put out two

scones, some butter and jam along with cups and saucers, and then prepared to hobble through to my office. But the lady helped.

'I'll carry that!' she said. 'You've enough, coping with your crutch.'

And so she bore the tray through the house and into my office. It was neat and tidy with lovely views across the dale, and I was delighted to have such a pleasant companion, if only for a cup of tea and a chat.

She placed the tray and its contents on one end of my desk as I settled in my usual chair. She found one against the far wall and hauled it across. When I had poured the tea and handed her a scone with a knife for the butter and another for the jam, we settled down for our meeting. Even at this point, I had no idea who she was or what she wanted.

'So,' I continued after the small talk involving our little party. 'How can I help you?'

'I'm not sure,' she began. 'Maybe it's not within the scope of your business but someone in the village suggested I come to see you.'

'Fire away! But first, might I ask your name? I've not noticed you around the village.'

'No, I live in Kent. Tunbridge Wells to be precise. I am Charlotte MacKenzie. Mrs,' she added after the briefest of pauses. 'I used to visit this part of England in my childhood, and I've often marvelled at how it is so much nicer than us southerners are led to believe. No coal mines, dark satanic mills, factories, back-to-back houses, grime . . . just lovely woods, rivers, moors and dales with open views and lots of fresh air.'

'We don't brag about it,' I laughed. 'We like to tell people it's all industrialized and horrible, it keeps unwanted folks away! Too many visitors would ruin it.'

'I'll keep your secret,' she smiled.

'So, tell me why you are here.'

'You may remember Miss Bromley. Helen Bromley. She lived in Sorrell Cottage at the foot of the dale here in Micklesfield.'

'Yes indeed, she died a few months ago. She held a life

policy with the Premier; it went into her estate upon her death. She was a lovely lady, most gentile and kind. She always insisted I had a cup of tea and a rock bun when I called.'

'I'm her niece, Mr Taylor. I'm not sure whether you knew any of her family, since most of us live in Kent and the Home Counties, but Aunt Helen insisted on living on these moors when she retired. She was a civil servant; she worked for the Home Office. She retired more than twenty-five years ago and loved it here. Like I say, I used to come and stay with her when I was a child. I took the train all the way from London by myself, and she would meet me in York in her little car and drive me out here. Quite wonderful. I've spent many happy hours at Sorrell Cottage – which is where I am staying now.'

'I knew the house hadn't been sold but had no idea what was happening to it.'

'My husband thinks we should keep it, Mr Taylor. I'm her only niece and there are no nephews; she left everything to me. Geoffrey – my husband – wants us to keep the cottage and use it ourselves for holidays or perhaps rent it to holidaymakers. It seems a shame to let it go after spending so many happy times there, and so I have agreed. We'll keep it.'

'It is a lovely place.'

I knew it well. It was a small two-storey house built in local stone with a blue slate roof, and it had a beautiful small garden with views overlooking the dale. It had once been a farm worker's cottage but had been sold to Helen Bromley some years ago when farmers began to employ fewer staff. The reduction in the number of farm workers was the inevitable result of mechanization, particularly combine harvesters, threshing machines and ploughs drawn by tractors instead of horses. Lots of similar small cottages came on to the market and were purchased by well-off people, often as a holiday home.

'There is one problem,' she said. 'It is full of Aunt Helen's little treasures, oddments she's collected over the years, things no-one wants these days. She never threw anything out, no matter how old it was, or how cracked or rusty or useless. There's knitting needles and pattern books by the score, cups and saucers, old pans and plates, birthday and Christmas presents she's never unwrapped and cards she's never thrown out, clothes she's never worn, wardrobes full of coats and dresses, shoes and slippers, letters still in their envelopes from friends and family, piles of magazines and newspapers, cracked plant pots and rusty gardening tools . . . You name it, Mr Taylor, and Aunt Helen has it stacked in and around her cottage. It's almost impossible to get inside because of all the stuff; I had to shift stacks of newspapers before I could reach the bed I'm using.'

By this stage I was beginning to wonder what on earth the condition of Aunt Helen's cottage had to do with me. On several occasions, I had been inside her cottage to collect her modest premium when she was alive, but had never ventured any further than the kitchen. There was always a fire blazing in the kitchen range and that's where we had enjoyed our tea and snack. Now, as I reflected upon those visits, I could recall the kitchen was always full of what might be loosely termed bric-a-brac. I remembered crowded shelves and work surfaces, stacks of things in boxes under the table, old flat irons by the score and more than one copper kettle.

'You'll be wondering what all this has to do with you?' She smiled mischievously at me.

'I am a little baffled,' I had to admit. 'I thought my links with Sorrell Cottage had ended with your aunt's death.'

'Let me explain a little further,' she said, sipping from her cup. I poured a second one for her with one for myself. 'Most of the stuff in her cottage is junk, Mr Taylor, I'm sure of that. I don't think we are likely to find any hidden treasures but one can never be sure. I have asked an auctioneer to value it with a view to taking it to a sale room, but he says that clearing the house and transporting everything to an auction would cost more than it would realize in a sale, especially with the auctioneer's commission to consider.

'He said it was worthless stuff and it would make much

more sense for me to clear it myself – simply to throw most of it away or burn it. Take it to the tip or get the dustman to cart it away.'

'I can understand that.'

'The snag is that it would take months, Mr Taylor, and I don't have that sort of time to spare. Also, it would cost a fortune to hire someone else to do the job. I am working, and these few days here are part of my annual holiday. I've very few holidays left and quite simply I haven't the time to spend on clearing the cottage. It would take months.'

'Go on.' I was still baffled by her need to talk this over with me.

'I want to hold a party at the cottage, a sort of junk and wine party. I thought that if I gave the stuff away, with glasses of wine as the inducement to attend, I might get rid of most of the clutter. It's amazing what people will accept if it's free.'

'It sounds a good idea, but the people around here aren't really wine drinkers.' I felt I had to add a note of caution to this plan.

'Exactly,' she said. 'So the wine will be something special. I would choose a day in high summer, with fine weather almost guaranteed, and everyone who came through the gate would be offered a glass of wine when they left, provided they took away anything they wanted, except for things I'd want to keep, like some of the furniture. I'd place that in a separate room, under lock and key! But they'd have to remove something to qualify for the free wine. They could take the stuff out by the handful, bag full, barrow load or cart load if necessary. If they came back for another glass of wine, they'd have to take another load away. I know some might only take a very small item, but knowing how human nature works, I'd guarantee some would take as much as they could carry, just because it's free.'

'That's true enough. Owt for nowt!'

'So that's my general idea. A sale without having to pay anything, and with free drinks thrown in! It must work. What I would pay for the wine would not be as much as paying for an auctioneer to clear the place, and it would encourage others to clear the house for me. They'd do all the work and have fun at the same time, perhaps hoping to find a treasure of some kind. I wouldn't expect everything to go of course, but I like to think most of it would – and I could cope with the remainder. A good bonfire will work wonders!'

'It sounds a brilliant idea!' I'd never come across this kind of dealing. 'It's a nice theory but are you sure it will work here in the North Yorkshire moors? Some of these folks are a bit canny and cautious, and they might suspect some kind of devious plot.'

'You always get people who think like that, but I believe it's worth a try. It worked for a friend of mine in Somerset,' she told me. 'He had a load of rusty gardening tools to get rid of in his father's shed, along with cracked plant pots, seed boxes, ancient wheelbarrows and so on, all useless and not worth a penny, so he organized a cider party and cleared the entire place in an afternoon. The only stipulation is that the drinker must take something away – he gave the visitors their cider as they were leaving with arms full of junk and most of them came back for more.'

'I think the local bobby should be told about this! We don't want Micklesfield to be full of drunks!'

'I know all the risks, but I'm prepared to give it a try, Mr Taylor, and of course, I would do all the right things. I can't sell the alcohol without the necessary licence so I will give it away to remain within the law, and I will inform the police and whoever else needs to be told. The more people who know about this plan, the better!'

'I'm sure you'd generate a house full of people! And there's plenty of space outside the house to cater for any traffic that might arrive. So what do you want from me?'

'Two things, Mr Taylor. First, I have heard about your new magazine and so I think it would be a good idea to put an advert in a prominent place to tell people about this. I know I have to come up with a firm date very soon, so one reason for my visit is to see if I'm in time for the next issue of the magazine. In fact, the very first issue, I believe?'

'Yes, it is the first and I hope it will set the pattern for the others, but I've a few weeks before the final deadline.

If you can draft the advert with the date and time, I can include it. The cost would depend upon the size of the advert – but whatever its shape and size, it will be cheaper than paying an auctioneer or house-clearer.'

'Good, then I shall go away and fix a day, then I'll come back to see you. But there is another matter.'

'Yes?'

'Insurance, Mr Taylor. If I am to invite the public on to my property for this kind of event, I feel I should take out a public liability policy, just in case someone gets hurt in the crush or trips over a stone in the garden and tries to sue me! I know this kind of insurance is popular in the south wherever a large crowd is likely to attend and it does give peace of mind. Is that something you can arrange?'

'Yes, of course. I'd need to know the date and times of opening once you've determined them, and because it would be for one day only, I think the premium would be quite low and acceptable, even if we have to anticipate a stampede. I can obtain more details from my District Office.'

'Good, then in the meantime I shall go away and do whatever is necessary, and I will return. And, Mr Taylor, my husband and I will need to have the cottage fully insured if we are to use it, or let it to holidaymakers. Is that something you can arrange?'

'If I were you, I'd have it comprehensively insured immediately, particularly as it's standing empty a lot of the time. It's always at risk even if you don't live there – everything from housebreakers to fires by way of gales, floods and, well, almost anything else.'

'Of course, I should have realized that. Can we do that too?'

'Rest assured I will see to it!' I told her before finding the necessary proposal form in my filing cabinet. She completed that before leaving and I said it would be mailed to District Office in that evening's post, and so she left to finalize the plans for her great free 'sale'.

Mrs MacKenzie later returned with the date and time of her big free sale, using for the advert's headline the Yorkshire phrase 'Summat for nowt'. When the great day eventually arrived, it was a huge success with people clamouring to gain entry to her cottage and later leaving with arms full of what others might describe as junk. One visitor turned out to be a collector of old newspapers and he managed to clear most of them, even forgoing the free wine on the grounds that he had to remain sober if he was to drive home. Others walked away with rusty tools, cracked crockery and an amazing number of things that no-one would normally consider having in their home. I began to wonder what on earth they would do with it all.

But I was successful too because I won two nice policies from that event, both with useful commission, one being for the day's risks – which produced no problems at all – and the second being a comprehensive policy for the house and remaining contents. I thought I had done quite well for a man who was supposed to be off work with a broken leg.

On another occasion, a farmer who was a client of mine had to put all his belongings and livestock up for sale, not because he wished to but because his waster of a son-in-law had brought the family's successful farming enterprise to the brink of bankruptcy. As the farmer in question felt that being declared bankrupt was the greatest shame that could befall him, he had decided to sell everything to pay off the debts. His name was Harold Atkinson and he farmed at High Barns, Baysthorpe.

The farm did not belong to Harold, however, for it was rented from Baysthorpe Estate and, as had been the custom for generations, the tenancy had been handed down from father to eldest son. Harold had therefore been born at the farm, lived there through his childhood and youth, and was now the tenant. Owning such premises had never occurred to him – almost all the farms in the dale belonged to large estates with hard-working tenants caring for them. That had been the way of life here for centuries.

Harold, a thoughtful and serious man in his mid-fifties, had always been a believer in insurance in case he was ill or any kind of disaster struck him, his family or his business. He had been a long-time client of the Premier, with me taking over his business from Jim Villiers, my predecessor. For that reason, I was a regular caller at the lonely farm, collecting premiums in cash once every month and sometimes advising him on new long-term policies that the Premier was promoting, particularly those with pensions for the self-employed in mind. But Harold did not have a son; his only child was a daughter, Angela, who had married a newcomer to the district, Brian Gaynes. Both in their early thirties, they were keen to continue the family tradition of farming at High Barns and so they lived in one end of the spacious farm house, occupying self-contained rooms which, in the past, had provided the accommodation for farm hands who lived-in. The purpose of this arrangement was for Brian and Angela to work the farm in equal partnership with Harold and his wife, Frances.

They would do so until Harold's retirement – which was not necessarily at the age of sixty-five. Some farmers worked well into their seventies and eighties but the age of the tenant did not affect such a change within a family. Whenever Harold retired, therefore, the youngsters would be skilled and sufficiently experienced to assume the tenancy and the Estate had agreed in principal to that proposal. In that way, the family tradition would be continued with great hopes that Angela would eventually produce a son. So far, there was no sign of that happy event although the partnership appeared to be working successfully because High Barns Farm, over the past few months, had begun to buy brand new and expensive machinery. As Harold had always been a rather cautious man who would never get into debt or even borrow from the bank, the arrival of a smart new family car became something of a talking point among his neighbours and friends. He must have been putting a few pounds away for years in order to afford it! The drama of that unexpected event continued when a new tractor appeared on the farm, along with extras such as a new Massey-Harris tractor-drawn self-binder and a tractor-powered belt-driven threshing machine. For Harold to buy just one of these items was unusual – to buy so many in such a short time was bordering on the miraculous and people began to wonder if he had won the football pools or, as some suggested, had suffered some kind of brainstorm.

The truth was none of those. The arrival of these expensive new items was Brian's idea. Being of the younger generation and having worked in a large construction business and then served in the Royal Navy during the war, Brian believed he had seen the world and the wisdom in what he called 'forward investment'. According to him, that meant borrowing money from the bank to finance the purchase of expensive new machinery. His theory was that it would, in the fullness of time, pay for itself with the increased turnover and larger profits which it helped to create. He also believed in visiting other regions, both in England and overseas, to study their farming techniques where, so he said, he could learn from the vast experience of others in a far wider market. For that reason, he took himself off, with Angela, to visit agricultural shows, spend time at open days at manufacturers' premises, attend demonstrations of new equipment, take part in seminars and courses and generally saturate himself in new methods and technology. With the war now behind them, the future looked wonderful and Brian was sure that entrepreneurs and risk-takers were vital to the new Britain.

The snag of course was that when Brian was away from the farm – which was increasingly the case – it meant Harold was left with all the work and worry, not least of which was meeting the high payments for the overdrafts and additional loans Brian had negotiated.

In simple terms, the output generated by Harold's farm gradually failed to generate the income necessary to pay the bills, which in turn meant that Harold had dug deep into his savings to ward off the evil day.

That day arrived when, for the first time in his life, Harold found himself unable to pay his creditors, one of which was the bank. News of his dilemma began to filter through to his friends and colleagues in the dale, and all had the greatest of sympathy for him. He was a thoroughly decent man and there is little doubt his new situation, which had not been brought about by himself, was causing him immense pain. He could be criticized for allowing Brian to have such a free hand in the running of the farm, and perhaps for being too trusting but, as he once said, it was a partnership. After all, Brian did have some good ideas for the future, including expansion of the farm and the production of new lines. There was even talk of turning one of the derelict barns into a holiday cottage to rent to tourists, but that conversion would also require a substantial loan from somewhere. But, as Harold had come to realize so painfully, Brian had gone too far too fast.

In time, the bank declined to extend the overdraft and called in the loan. Bankruptcy threatened. For Harold this was devastating and humiliating, but for the more worldly Brian it was normal business practice – he told Harold they could talk to another bank manager and seek another loan over a longer period, literally to buy more time to meet the demands now being forced upon them. But Harold was having none of this.

Fortunately, when the partnership agreement had been drawn up by Harold's solicitor, it contained a clause allowing Harold and his wife, as the nominated tenants, to make the final decisions in the event of a dispute, a state designed to prevail until Harold's eventual retirement.

And so Harold made his decision. He would avoid bankruptcy and further expensive loans by selling up. All his equipment and livestock would be auctioned to pay off the existing debts and he would leave the farm without being declared bankrupt. Whether Brian took up the vacant tenancy would then be his decision because the partnership would have been dissolved. If Brian continued with the farm he'd have to do so without Harold, and always with the Estate in the background keeping a close eye on matters. They would be anxious due to his lack of farming experience and it was generally felt in the dale that the Estate was not very happy with the way Brian had conducted his first foray into the farming world. It was hoped he had learned a lesson

but there was a feeling that he was not prepared to spend
time learning the craft from his expert father-in-law. He'd
rushed into the business headlong without any wish to
absorb the real skills and advance planning which were
necessary. The climax of this local saga occurred whilst I
was off work and I heard about it one morning when I
managed to struggle up to the shop for some groceries.

'It's a rum do about awd 'Arold at High Barns,' said an
aged gent who had popped in for a tin of ready-rubbed
tobacco.

'Why, what's happened?' asked Roger Crossley, the
shopkeeper.

'Selling up to avoid going bust.'

'Not Harold Atkinson, surely? Harold from High Barns
at Baysthorpe? That Harold?'

'Aye, him, the very same.'

I joined the fray. 'But he's never owed a penny to anybody.
He never borrows money, always pays cash on the nail . . .
I've never had to wait for my money, not that I take very
much off him!'

'Aye, but it's that son-in-law of his, spending all his
money on fancy ideas and new tractors and stuff, and
leaving awd 'Arold to pick up the pieces. 'Arold's been
working night and day to try and make ends meet. 'E
should 'ave 'ad more sense than to take him on. Shame
really, 'Arold's one of the world's nicest chaps, a real gent.'

I must admit I was shocked at the news simply because
Harold Atkinson was one of the most hard-working men in
the dale – diligent, skilful, kind-hearted, uncomplaining,
helpful to his friends and neighbours . . . all kinds of praise
could be heaped upon his head and so this news would
shock everyone. It was while walking slowly home down
the hill, doing my best to ease my pot leg gingerly before
me, that I recalled Evelyn saying Frances Atkinson had not
had the monthly premium ready for collection when she'd
called last week. At the time, it meant nothing – Frances
usually paid out of her egg money – but now it did mean
something. I must admit I walked home with a heavy heart,
uncertain whether to believe the news without more proof,

but at the same time recognizing the warning signs. Although I could not recall him missing a payment to me, I must check my books to see whether Harold was behind with his premiums, and also make discreet enquiries at other places such as local garages and shops.

I began to wonder whether he had been avoiding payment of his regular bills or whether his wife had not been paying them. And then I thought about his new car, tractor and machinery, and that son-in-law who never seemed to do a bit of work around the farm. Back in my office, I checked my records and found that Harold was up to date with all his policies, except last week's. In addition to a life insurance policy for him and his wife, his household effects, vehicles, machinery and some special livestock – a bull and a stallion – were insured with the Premier. I must admit I began to wonder whether the story of his problems was nothing more than a rumour and then there was a knock on my back door. When I opened it, Harold himself was standing there, cap in hand.

'Now then, Mr Taylor,' he began. He always called me Mr Taylor even though I called him Harold; I think it was something to do with the fact I wore a suit for work. 'Can I have a word?'

'Of course, Harold, come in.' I led him through to my office and settled him on a chair but he refused my offer of a cup of tea. 'So how can I help you?'

'I don't think anybody can help me, Mr Taylor, not now. You might have heard.'

'Heard what?' I pretended to be ignorant. After all, I wasn't sure what he was going to tell me.

'I'm selling up,' he said, wringing his cap like a dish cloth. 'The lot. Cows, sheep, pigs, hens, geese, tractor, trailers, implements . . . the lot. All going, Mr Taylor. Me and Frances will be moving out of the farm but we don't know where we're going yet. There's a lot to decide.'

'Like an early retirement?' I tried to appear none too concerned for I did not know how to respond.

'Nay, lad, worse than that. To save myself going bust. Which is why I'm here now. I'm telling all them I do business with, and that includes you. I shan't need them insurances, Mr Taylor, for the vehicles and machinery but I hope I can keep the life insurances going for me and the missus. Here's last week's premium, we missed it when your wife called. Half a crown.' And he plonked the coin on my desk.

'It could have waited, Harold.'

'Nay it couldn't, I don't believe in owing money.'

'I'm sorry, Harold, really I am.'

'My own daft fault, Mr Taylor, I was too trusting. I let our Angela's lad have a free reign; he said he could generate business for us, make us more money if only we got modernized . . . Well, it doesn't work like that, you can't put old heads on young shoulders, Mr Taylor, and I don't want to see my name in the bankruptcy courts so I'm selling up. I'll pay all my debts, you mark my words. Angela and that feller of hers will go their own way, we're ending the partnership. That's me finished with farming.' I detected a tremor in his voice as he said those final words.

His life's work was now over through the actions of someone else and I thought he was taking it all very calmly.

'I don't know what to say, Harold.'

'There's nowt you can say, Mr Taylor. It's over, all bar the formalities. We sell up in six weeks' time, on the Saturday, at High Barns. Last Saturday of next month. There'll be bargains for some. Anyroad, I thought I better come and tell you and get up to date with that life insurance, then we can cancel t'others.'

'I think we should wait until the sale is concluded,' I said. 'Six weeks is a long time and you need to be insured in the meantime. I can wait for the premiums, don't worry about that, it can all come out of the proceeds of your sale.'

'Aye, mebbe you're right. But I thought you ought to know all the same.'

'Thank you, I appreciate you coming to tell me.'

'Aye, well, it's not easy, telling folks. But I don't believe in hiding from the truth. Life has to go on and so it will.' He wrung his cap even more tightly as he rose to his feet. 'I'll be off then.'

'I'll watch out for the notices of the sale,' I said. 'I might manage to get along if this leg's better by then.'

'Everybody else will be there, Mr Taylor. Not that I mind 'em coming along for a good poke around my stuff, but if there's a good crowd it might make 'em bid a bit higher for things.'

'I hope it all works out, Harold, for you and Frances, really I do.'

'Aye,' he said and left.

When he'd gone I made a note to remind myself to enter his payment in my collecting book, currently out on its rounds with Evelyn, and then jotted the date in my diary, thinking I might get along to the sale. When Evelyn came home, I told her about Harold's visit and she then told me that when Frances had been unable to find any money in the house, she had cried. Evelyn had offered to put in the half-crown so that the books were up to date, but Frances had asked her not to. 'I want to settle this myself, Mrs Taylor,' she'd insisted.

In the weeks that followed, news of Harold's problems had filtered to everyone in Delverdale; people in every village from the top to bottom of the dale knew him and respected him. All were shocked at this sudden and dreadful change in his affairs and all vowed to attend the sale. I am now jumping ahead with the tale because, when my leg was out of plaster, I was able to attend. When I arrived and parked in the field set aside as a car park, I realized the place was absolutely packed with potential purchasers. The sale, due to begin at 11 a.m., was to start inside a Dutch barn due to the uncertainty of the moorland weather.

The barn contained the small tools and implements used on the farm – saws, chisels, hammers, tins of screws, nuts and bolts, spanners and welding equipment, garden tools, ladders, muck forks, buckets, scythes and even some old flails, milk churns, a real miscellany of items, some very useful but others from a bygone age. By tradition, those lots were always sold first. Most of the other items had been arranged out of doors, next for sale being the larger farm equipment and machinery which stood in long rows around a field. Among them I spotted a tractor, binder, several ploughs, a harrow, a turnip-cutting machine, pig creel and several horse-drawn vehicles such as carts and even an ancient stone roller. Everyone would follow the auctioneer into the field to enjoy this experience and when all those items were sold, everyone would troop back into the buildings where fitments like oil tanks, hayracks and flour milling machinery would go under the hammer. Finally, it would be the turn of the livestock with the cattle, sheep, pigs and poultry all waiting patiently in their pens. They were the last to be auctioned, unless any household goods such as furniture or clothing were to be included. They would be sold from the house, the final part of the sale.

During the pre-sale activity, I spotted Harold among the crowd but did not have a word with him; he was far too busy with the auctioneer, officials and attendants. Also I noticed a large number of local farmers of the wealthier type, including Lord Baysthorpe, owner of Harold's farm.

The auction began promptly and I thought it appeared rather slow at the start with bidders perhaps feeling as if they were removing Harold's livelihood from him and his family, but soon it picked up. Although the prices appeared very modest, they were reasonable, particularly in view of the age and condition of some of the dead stock lots. This was especially the case with Harold's old tools, machinery and implements. With his traditional expertise, Paul Richardson, the auctioneer who lived in Micklesfield, worked his way through the catalogue, knocking some lots down to what I felt was a very low price. I wondered if there would be sufficient income for Harold to settle his debts, although I must admit I bought nothing. At such a sale, there was nothing I wished to buy!

Then after the last lot had been sold, a strange thing happened. Paul Richardson, in his powerful auctioneer's voice, called for silence. I noticed that no-one had gone home, neither had any of the lots been removed from the farm. Even the animals remained in their pens. Paul called for silence and said that Lord Baysthorpe wished to speak to everyone. His Lordship, a striking moustachioed figure in his plus fours and tweed jacket, climbed on to the auctioneer's rostrum and hit the woodwork with the gavel.

'We all know why we are here, even if Harold doesn't,' he said, and everyone cheered. I had no idea what was going on. He then located Harold somewhere in the crowd, hiding at the back in his sorrow, and continued.

'Harold, you are our friend, a friend to everyone in this place today and one of my best tenants. We know what has happened to you through no fault of your own, and all I can say now is that everything you see before you is yours again. The sale has generated enough to satisfy your bank – your bank manager is here – but no-one wishes to take away anything they have bought. Everything is returned to you, with our compliments and, of course, the farmhouse and land is yours for as long as you need it.'

Harold could not believe what was happening as he was ushered forward through the crowd to take his place beside Lord Baysthorpe, but he couldn't say a word. After a struggle, he managed a very hoarse 'I don't know what to say' before his words were drowned in cheers, but there was much patting of his back as he wiped away uncharacteristic tears.

And so, thanks to their peers, Harold and Frances Atkinson were able to continue farming.

I was so pleased I hadn't cancelled their insurance policies.

Five

'This evening at 7 p.m. there will be hymn singing in the field opposite the chapel. Please bring a blanket and be prepared to sin.'

From a chapel notice board

E velyn had left the house shortly before nine-thirty to go collecting in Walstone and Sutherdale with my usual advice as to where and how she would locate any premiums left in strange places. I hoped she would find Mrs Turner's two shillings in the left-hand nest box of her henhouse, and Mr Coleman's one and sixpence in the fork of his only apple tree. As usual, baby Paul had been spirited away to play with his cousin at Maureen's; it meant she could get on with her own chores whilst leaving the two children to play happily and safely, either in the garden or in the house.

I was therefore left to my own devices; there was nothing of importance or urgency in the morning post and my efforts with the village magazine were progressing very slowly. In fact, it was rather too slowly for my liking. Although the concept of producing a village magazine sounds quite simple, it was surprisingly time-consuming. The main problem was convincing volunteer contributors, who had promised a feature of some kind, that there really was a sense of modest urgency for delivery of their material. Some had no idea of the work involved in preparing contributions to meet a deadline, a matter of importance to a printer who himself had deadlines to meet in spite of other pressing commitments.

Some of the villagers whom I had approached for arti-cles or newsy pieces appeared to believe that if they wrote down the basics of an idea, either I or the printer would do the rest. It was not easy convincing them otherwise, especially in a manner that would not offend them. People could be surprisingly sensitive in such matters and some were liable to treat well-meaning advice as a form of criticism, particularly when it came from someone much younger than them.

Already I had found people could be very touchy about the quality of their work. Overt criticism was definitely unwise, even if they produced the most dreadful poems or worst prose in the belief that others would find their work enthralling. I was beginning to realize that working as editor of even the most modest of village magazines was tougher than I had anticipated. I began to experience sympathy with newspaper editors and those who produced magazines by the week or month. Dealing with the intricacies of insurance was much more straightforward! I had no trouble compiling a factual report about a claim following a traffic accident, the loss of a valuable piece of jewellery or a housebreaking in a fashionable home. However, I had promised the vicar I'd fulfil the role of editor at least for this first edition, and so I bent to the task.

It was while wading through the pile of unedited ideas and notes, some of which I might be able to knock into shape, that my telephone rang. It was Father O'Hagan from St Eulalia's Roman Catholic Church at Graindale Bridge.

'Ah, Matthew my friend,' Father O'Hagan began in his strong Irish brogue. 'To be sure I'm glad I caught you.'

'Morning Father,' I responded. 'It's a very nice morning, so how can I help you?'

'I hope I haven't caught you at an awkward time, I know you must be very busy, even with that broken leg of yours. How is it coming along, by the way?'

'Fine,' I responded. 'I can get about better than I expected. I'm hoping to get the plaster off fairly soon, but I'm still unable to drive the car so Evelyn is doing my collecting in the dale. I think she's enjoying the change of scenery and the chance to meet other people.'

'Good for her; she's a real treasure, Matthew. You're a

lucky fellow, so you are. Now, the reason for my call. I think I need some insurance.'

'You *think* you do?'

'Yes, I think I do, but I'm not sure. You could advise me, perhaps?'

'Well, that is something I can do. I can talk and offer advice, broken leg or no broken leg.'

'So if you can't drive yet, then perhaps I should come along to see you? I have to visit a sick parishioner in Micklesfield later today, Mrs Young from High Terrace, so perhaps I could call on you?'

'Yes, that would be convenient. I'm at home all day.'

'Maybe just after dinner time, Matthew? Two-thirty or so?'

'Fine, so what type of insurance do you require? Is there something I can be preparing or researching before you arrive?'

'It's for a relic,' he said.

'A relic? What sort of relic?'

'A relic of St Eulalia,' he said. 'Very precious. She's the patron saint of our church, as you know. I'll tell you all about it when I see you. Two-thirty, then?'

'Yes, I'll have the kettle on.'

'God bless you, Matthew.' And with that he rang off.

At this stage, I had no idea what the relic might be or whether it was valuable, but I did know the Premier had no specialist insurance policy for saintly relics. Nonetheless, the company did insure the contents of some of the country's finest museums and art galleries. That meant it did not shy away from covering ancient and historic objects which might not have any great monetary value but which may be irreplaceable as items of local, national or international importance. The Premier's policies covered everything from ancient fossils to valuable works of art, and this broad range extended to the contents of private houses. Many people owned highly sentimental objects that would have no commercial value on the open market but which were irreplaceable. I wondered if Father O'Hagan's relic was such a thing – valueless from a fiscal viewpoint but important from a religious one.

The Premier was large enough and wise enough to insure such things, usually giving them a low nominal value, but the relic of a saint was something out of the ordinary. I wondered how District Office would view this proposal when it was submitted, but I could not seek positive advice in advance because I had no idea what the relic might be. Could it be something as sombre as a piece of bone or hair, or might it be St Eulalia's prayer book, rosary beads or something very holy and venerable? A letter perhaps? An item of clothing? I could only wait and see.

During my wait for the priest, his call reminded me of a case a few months earlier when I had to insure a house and contents in Great Freyerthorpe dale. Once a game-keeper's cottage and owned by Freyerthorpe Estate, the house was almost at the head of the dale, tucked away along a rough track. It was sheltered by the bulk of the heathery moorland, which towered behind it with no other house in view. Remote but beautiful, it was constructed of local stone and was a substantial structure with four bedrooms, spacious living accommodation, plenty of outbuildings and nearly an acre of land, much of it cultivated. No longer required by the estate because of a reduction in their staffing numbers, it had been placed on the open market. It had been purchased by a Mr and Mrs Lucas – Ralph and Lorna – who owned a textile mill near Halifax in the West Riding of Yorkshire. They were wealthy enough to pay cash for the cottage and were semi-retired, with their son now in charge of the mill and Ralph popping into the office once a week or so.

He owned a car but his real love was the open moorland around his home where he painted in oils and studied the folklore and wildlife of the area; his earlier hard work and business acumen had enabled him to indulge in his hobbies, something Lorna also enjoyed. She was an expert in the botany of the moors and was in demand as a speaker on the subject. They were a charming and friendly couple who regarded themselves as fortunate to live in such an idyllic area.

It was no coincidence, therefore, that their house was called Witch Post Cottage. It was known by that name simply

because it contained a witch post, one of several properties in Delverdale and Eskdale that also boasted this kind
of unusual feature. They were called witch posts because
no-one really knew what they were or why they had been
incorporated into the fabric of just a few houses.

Ralph's interest in the folklore of the moors had convinced
him he should buy the cottage, if only because it featured
a witch post, but it also prompted him to conduct more
research into other houses that contained such curiosities.
It was known that there were around twenty other witch
posts in and around the North York Moors. They existed
nowhere else, other than two in Lancashire. In Ralph's view,
there may have been others in properties within the moorland area, some perhaps having been removed or destroyed
in modernization schemes and others perhaps hidden
beneath new structures. Some might still exist but many
could have been removed and lost forever without anyone
really knowing what they were – or perhaps not caring.

According to popular belief, a witch post was a type of
charm which would prevent witches from casting evil spells
on the house and its occupants, whether human or animal.
The presence of the post would deter the witches and prevent
any evil spells they might cast upon the place – or that was
the theory. The posts known to still exist had been installed
during the seventeenth century when the fear of witches
and witchcraft was at its height, particularly in remote rural
areas. In addition to the posts, however, the occupants took
other measures to safeguard themselves against witches.
They used dozens of charms ranging from horseshoes
hanging on the doors, the growth of elder trees near the
buildings, the burial of witch bottles under the threshold,
the use of rowan wood for their household utensils and
tools, along with lots of other charms and rituals. In remote
Yorkshire, for example, it was said that 'If your whipstock
is made of rowan wood, you may ride your nag through
any town.'

There is no proof, however, that these intriguing posts
were actually installed to deter witches; it is simply a theory
because no other purpose seemed obvious. A witch post is

nothing more than a strong pillar of wood, invariably oak, which stands on the floor of the kitchen and supports the smoke hood of the fireplaces of the period, usually the seventeenth century or thereabouts. Some six or eight feet tall, the pillar is identified as a witch post because the front edge – that facing into the kitchen – bears elaborate carvings, the centre piece of which is a cross like an X.

In some cases, a date was included with the carving – one from Postgate Farm at Glaisdale, for example, bears the date 1664 and the initials EPIB.

Ralph's theory, however, was that these were not witch posts at all, but marks made by a travelling Catholic priest in the penal times. The cross depicted on the posts does not match any kind of normal witch-deterring mark or charm; it is more like the crosses used in Catholic devotion worldwide, and in some countries the letter X represents Christ. The X-shaped cross is also the emblem of St Andrew, the patron saint of Scotland and many other countries. He was crucified on a cross of that shape, which is familiar through its use on the Scottish flag, and indeed on the Union Jack. In the case of the Postgate Farm post, the initials could be the first letters of a Latin prayer or hymn. It had long been customary in the Catholic church to use such abbreviations for short Latin prayers, perhaps the best known examples being RIP – *requiescat in pace* – otherwise known as 'rest in peace', or DG, meaning *Deo gratias*. There are others.

It is possible, therefore, that these posts were secret indicators within selected premises to indicate where Mass could safely be celebrated by a Catholic priest travelling from house to house during the Penal time. They might also be an indication that the house in question had been blessed by a Catholic priest.

To add support to this theory, there was such a priest travelling around the moors during that period. He was Father Nicholas Postgate, who was cruelly executed at York in 1679 for baptising a child into the Catholic faith. He worked in secret and in disguise on the moors between 1630 and 1679 – around the same time that those so-called witch posts were being installed. There is no proof that Postgate Farm at Glaisdale is named after the martyr, however. Postgate is an old name for locations in and around the moors and it means 'a road marked by posts'. There is a nearby hamlet called Stonegate and the term 'gate' also features in the street names in many northern towns and cities.

I found Ralph's knowledge and theories fascinating and he had explained his ideas when he arrived a few months earlier to insure Witch Post Cottage and its contents. It was when we got around to listing the valuable house contents, such as his collection of oil paintings and some antique furniture, that he mentioned the witch post and provided me with his theories. I wasn't sure how it might feature in an insurance policy.

'It's more of a fixture than part of the contents,' I had to point out. 'It's an essential part of the structure because it's holding up the smoke hood of the fireplace, just as a cross-beam or lintel might hold up essential parts of the building. I can imagine my bosses ruling that it is nothing more than a supporting pillar which happens to have some interesting carving on it. It was probably installed before the carving appeared, in which case it is merely a wooden post and therefore not subject to special insurance cover.'

'You surprise me, Mr Taylor. I thought the Premier would recognize something that is clearly very precious and unique.'

'I'm sure the Premier's advisers would suggest the carving is both interesting and of some historical significance but, as for insurance, they would argue that anything could have been carved on that piece of wood. Lovers' initials, the name of the house, anything at all and, to be honest, no-one knows what those witch posts really are or why they are there.'

'So if Constable had painted his original Haywain picture on my kitchen wall, would that be a mere fitting or fixture?' he asked. 'Or if we found some medieval carvings in the stonework?'

'I don't know how our experts assess this kind of thing.' I was honest with him. 'Having listened to what you have told me, I think we should declare the witch post on the proposal form, highlighting its rather unique role, but we will also need to state its value.'

'Value? You can't put a value on something like this, Mr Taylor. It's part of our cultural and religious history.'

'It has *some* value,' I said. 'It might find a sale for a few shillings as a nice piece of seasoned oak. That's how the police operate when they have to put a price on something which has been stolen, something with only sentimental value. They simply record the basic cost of the materials from which it is made.'

'So you're saying the Premier would only insure my witch post for the price of the timber it's made from?'

'I think in your case it would be considered an integral part of the structure and not assessed individually, therefore I doubt if a valuation would be necessary. Before you bought Witch Post Cottage, the house was insured by the estate with no special reference to the witch post.'

'I can understand that. But can't we nominate it as a work of art? It *is* a work of art, it's a carving or a sculpture, probably Jacobean and very skilfully done. I don't want it lost, Mr Taylor. If something happens to my house after I've gone to meet my Maker, I don't want the witch post removed or destroyed.'

'I hardly think insuring it will prevent later buyers from removing it, or giving it to a museum . . .'

'I wouldn't object to that . . . in fact, I think it's a great idea. The museum suggestion, I mean. It would then be safe for the future, even if it means removing something precious from my house's history.'

'Then you'd have to include it in your will, Mr Lucas, or make it a condition of any future sale of your property – but you're not destined for the grave just yet. I think you should take photographs of it too, just for the record. Look, we will complete the proposal form now, giving due prominence to the witch post, and I'm sure it will feature in the policy as an object of special interest. I will include a note pointing out the unique nature of the feature.'

And so we completed the necessary proposal form for

comprehensive insurance of Witch Post Cottage, its contents and its special feature.

No value was placed upon the witch post, other than to state it was an unusual historic feature of the property, and no additional premium was added to the cost of the insurance. To my knowledge, it was never removed because successive owners have always wanted to retain it in its original form and situation, something Mr Lucas had stipulated as an alternative to placing it in a museum. Another thing for me to consider, of course, was a feature about witch posts in the *Micklesfield Magazine*, but I felt the subject justified more space than I might have available in the first issue. I felt sure Mr Lucas would write and illustrate the piece if I asked him.

It was with those curious and very localized objects in mind that I awaited with interest the arrival of St Eulalia's relic. One thing that had always puzzled me was why this remote church in the Yorkshire moors had adopted Eulalia as its patron saint. The church was fairly modern, little more than 150 years old, having been built for the Catholics in the dale who had retained their ancient faith in spite of the Reformation. Its devoted parishioners always made a great fuss about celebrating St Eulalia's day on 10 December but I had never heard about a relic being used in any of the ceremonies. So far as I was aware, the church did not possess any relics of St Eulalia.

Another puzzle about adopting this saint is that she was Spanish and the member of a wealthy family. When Eulalia was a twelve-year-old maiden living in Merida, the town's prefect was actively persecuting Christians so Eulalia rebuked him for his part in those atrocities. She also attacked a pagan idol and threw it to the ground whereupon she was immediately arrested, tortured and burned to death.

One legend associated with her death was that a dove emerged from her mouth at the point of death and flew up to heaven, and another was that an untimely fall of snow covered her wrecked body. Some believers thought the dove was really her departing soul. The year of her martyrdom was AD 303 or 304. Other than these few facts, little is known about Eulalia. Clearly, I was highly intrigued about what the relic might be, particularly as some 1650 years had passed since her cruel death in Spain. Once again, I thought it might make a subject for the magazine, but I needed to know much more about Eulalia.

When Father O'Hagan arrived, he was carefully carrying a cardboard box stuffed with tissue paper. He placed it gingerly on my desk and opened it to lift out the tissue paper and its hidden contents. As he removed the paper, I could see what looked like a yellowish-grey coloured pot with carvings all around it. It had a flat base and a domed lid held in position by a metal clasp. The lid was also covered with similar carvings. The entire pot was about eight inches high with a diameter of some four or five inches.

With great care and a show of reverence, the priest placed it on my desk and then settled on the chair I had placed ready for him.

'There you are, Matthew. How about that?' Clearly, he was proud of his trophy.

'What is it?'

'That's a very good question, but whatever it is, it's a relic of our patron saint, Eulalia.'

'It looks like a large snuff jar or even a jam pot, or perhaps an urn of some sort,' I said. 'Is the relic inside?'

'No, it's empty, this pot is the relic.'

'Oh.' I had expected something different, perhaps a lock of hair, a piece of her clothing or even a sliver of bone. It would not have surprised me to find it kept in such a container. 'So how old is this pot?'

'Well, Eulalia lived in the fourth century, which makes it sixteen hundred years old or more.'

'Have you had it valued? Or assessed in any way? By an expert?

'Oh no, Matthew. I wouldn't want it to be handled more than was necessary; genuine holy relics are hard to come by.'

'And you want it insured?'

'I think it must be insured, Matthew. As you know, some of our church artefacts are insured through your good self and the Premier – the candlesticks, the monstrance, the crucifix, chalice, silverware, oak furnishings and so on.'

'Yes, we have a standard policy for churches, that's no problem, and we do insure the contents of quite a few churches who are not Church of England, who tend to use a dedicated insurance group, but this is different. Is it your intention to have it on display in the church?'

'Oh, yes, I think we must. It's a direct link with our patron saint, Matthew; we can't hide it from the people.'

'My superiors will want to know where it is to be kept and I think if it proves to be valuable from a financial aspect, they would want it to be made very secure. It is possible to get very strong cabinets which enable important objects to be placed on view to the public but can also keep them safe from damage or theft.'

'You are not suggesting someone would steal from a church, are you?'

'Perhaps that would never have happened in the past, Father, but things are changing. There are those who would cheerfully steal from a church, as we know from some of the claims processed by the Premier. Silverware from the altar, ancient candlesticks and even furniture like chairs and benches can be targeted, to say nothing of breaking into offertory boxes.'

'But that is sacrilege!'

'So it is, but the thieves don't see it like that. They see things which are easily transported and which can be sold very quickly to people who don't ask too many questions. And cash from offertory boxes is always wanted by thieves. Sadly, though, they do take quite rare and valuable things in some cases. So, Father, the short answer is that I will submit a proposal form with a detailed description of this pot, which you must sign, and then we will sit back and await the decision of my seniors and assessors. The more questions I can answer before we submit the proposal, though, the more likely it is we shall have an easy passage with this rather unusual item.'

'All right. I understand, so what do you want to know?'

Prior to his arrival, I had located the necessary proposal form and it was in my pending tray, awaiting the details only Father O'Hagan could provide.

'I need to describe it in as much detail as possible, even with the maker's name and something that will help us to value it; a photograph might be a good idea too.'

'I have some; I got Philip to take them last week. He's one of our parishioners, as you know, very good with a camera.' He delved into his jacket pocket and pulled out a folder containing a few small snapshots, all in black and white but with nothing to suggest the scale of the pot. That was not too important, as I could provide its measurements when completing the proposal form.

'That's good, I'll include a selection. Now, Father, I need to know where it came from and I need to know how we can prove its age and authenticity.'

'Well, it has just come into my possession, not my personal possession I must stress, but the church's possession. I am its custodian until I leave here.'

'So how do you know it is a relic of St Eulalia?'

'Because it says so in the will of the lady who left it to the church. It has been in her family for generations. Now, Matthew, you might not know, but the very first priest of St Eulalia's, more than a hundred and fifty years ago, had a Spanish grandmother.'

'I've often wondered why you adopted Eulalia.'

'It was his suggestion. His grandfather was English and his father and mother were English, but in past generations he had Spanish blood in his veins, on the female side. And those Spanish senoras, going back over the centuries, were given that pot. It had once belonged to a distant relation of theirs.'

'So its history will be difficult to trace?'

'Well, the story is that the distant relation was a very distant relation of St Eulalia's family, and that this pot had been passed down the family through all those generations. That's the story as it was told to me. Now you can see why our church at Graindale Bridge is called St Eulalia's.'

'But there is no proof it belonged either to Eulalia or her family, is there?'

'Proof? There is the family history, Matthew, word of mouth from good-living people down the generations and probably more reliable than any piece of paper.'

'I am playing Devil's advocate here. I am thinking of the questions which our assessors might ask if we claim it is the genuine relic of a saint.'

'Don't forget, Matthew, that it bears carvings of white doves, of the very kind that are supposed to have flown to heaven from the mouth of the dying Eulalia.'

'Doves, are they? Those carvings?'

'Yes, all over the pot. Take a closer look.'

I bent to examine it more closely, first lifting it carefully to look beneath to see if there were any indications of a date, or maker's name or country of origin, but there were none. There was nothing inside either, and in fact once the lid was raised, it looked surprisingly clean and undamaged in its interior. When I looked more carefully at the exterior, though, I could see that the carvings, in relief, were all doves in various positions, some intertwined with others, some perched among leaves and others in flight. There was just a possibility that what I interpreted as leaves might have been flames – and Eulalia had been burned to death – but apart from that I saw nothing to suggest the pot had been made with a saintly memory or a martyr's death in mind. There were no holy images – no crosses, no figures of Christ or the angels, no female figure that might have been Eulalia.

I was thinking it might have been commissioned after her death, as a kind of memento, rather than belonging to her when she was alive. And it might have then contained something of hers, a relic of some kind – even ashes if she had been burned to death.

'It's not made of clay or porcelain, is it?' I asked next.

'No, it's ivory. Carved ivory with a metal fastener.'

'Father, if those doves represent the one which is said to have flown from Eulalia's mouth at the moment of her death, then this pot could not have belonged to her, could it? The doves apparently appeared at the moment of her death; it was her death which produced that famous dove. That means this pot might have belonged to her family. I believe they were well-to-do; they might have commissioned the pot to her memory.'

'I can't answer that, Matthew; I don't have that kind of detailed knowledge.'

'All I can do, Father, is put a précis of this information on the proposal form and wait for the response from my District Office. It will take a few days.'

'And in the meantime, what happens to this relic?'

'I think you should take it away and look after it very carefully, and the moment I have some news, I'll be in touch. I'd like you to bear in mind that one of our expert assessors might wish to examine the pot.'

'That will not be a problem, Matthew, I won't lock it away.'

'Good. In the meantime, I will endorse the file to ensure the pot is insured from this moment, even though we have not yet determined its authenticity or value.'

'Thank you.'

As we concluded our conversation, I got the impression he was not very pleased with my questioning, probably thinking I was casting grave doubts on the authenticity of the pot. In my view, he appeared convinced it was a genuine relic but I knew, and he would know, that in the past it was the custom of witnesses at the execution of martyrs or famous villains to grab a piece of something belonging to the victim. They would do their utmost to acquire items like a glove or a piece of clothing, or else they wanted something used in the execution itself such as a piece of the rope, the axe handle or even a splinter of blood-stained wood or a handful of blooded earth. So far as religious martyrs were concerned, their followers always tried to remove something from the place of martyrdom and take it home with them.

Thus, there are thousands of pieces of the True Cross, the very cross upon which Christ was crucified, and they can be found in churches across the world – and there used to be a good international trade in the relics of holy martyrs, not only in Christian churches. But who now knows whether or not such artefacts are genuine? The stories are easy to pass between one generation and another and because they come from family members, they are accepted as genuine.

Father O'Hagan left, taking his precious pot with him, and I promised to get in touch the moment I had some news from District Office. After a week or so, I received a telephone call from Leonard Evans, the District Manager of the Premier at its Ryethorpe offices.

'Ah, Mr Taylor,' he breezed down the phone. 'And how is the leg this morning?'

'Coming along nicely, thank you,' I responded. 'I expect to be going to hospital soon for a check-up.'

'Good, well, don't let them rush things, it's better to be safe than sorry, and I know your wife is doing a wonderful job for us in your Delverdale agency. But I'm not ringing about that, Mr Taylor; it's about this proposal form for the saint's relic, if indeed that's what it is. We have examined the photographs, Mr Taylor, but before we commit ourselves to a policy of insurance, our district assessor, Mr Linden, Frank Linden that is, would like to examine the pot in question. The photographs are very good, but he would like to see it in real life.'

'I alerted the priest to that possibility,' I said.

'Good. Then I shall telephone him to make an appointment for us to make an expert assessment of the pot, and we would like you to be present.'

'I can't drive yet . . .' I began.

'Not to worry, I will collect you when I drive our district assessor to Graindale Bridge. Will next Tuesday afternoon be a problem, if I can fix a time?'

'No, not at all.'

And so it was that on Tuesday I found myself being helped into Mr Evans' car with some ungainly movements and eventually settled on the rear seat with my leg spanning the width of the floor space. Father O'Hagan was expecting us and had alerted his housekeeper to prepare a tray of afternoon tea and biscuits. Armed with briefcases, therefore, we were shown into his study, a cosy book-lined room with a coal fire burning beneath a massive crucifix that hung above the mantelpiece, and on a side table stood the ivory pot.

'Can I pick it up?' asked Linden.

'Yes,' said Father O'Hagan, if a little reluctantly.

'I'll be most careful,' Linden promised.

Holding it in the slender fingers of both hands, Linden turned it over, peered at the carved doves through a magnifying glass, lifted the lid and tested the hinges and fastener, weighed it in his hands and then nodded.

'Hmm,' he said as he replaced the precious object on the priest's table. 'Have a look at these, Father.'

He opened his briefcase and extracted some enlarged photographs which, to an untrained eye like mine, looked identical to Father O'Hagan's pot. He passed them to the priest.

'This, Father, is not your pot, although I would suggest, had I not told you that, you might have thought it was. It's identical in shape, size and design.'

'Really?' Father O'Hagan peered closely at the photos and then nodded. 'I'd say that was my pot.'

'This one is in the museum of the Hispanic Society of America, Father. It is a Hispano-Moresque ivory box dating back to the tenth century. Yours is identical.'

'Tenth century, you say?'

'Yes, which means yours could not be as early as the death of St Eulalia. She died in AD 303 or 304, six centuries or so earlier.'

'Ah,' was all the priest could say, the disappointment clear on his face.

'But,' continued Mr Linden, 'there is every reason for believing Eulalia inspired these pots, as she is known especially for the story of the dove and for being roasted to death. I think flames are shown on the pots. She was Spanish, as you know, but devotion to her spread to Africa, Gaul and Italy, and she is even mentioned by the venerable Bede in his hymn to St Etheldreda. So there we are. You have a very rare piece of ivory here, Father and, according to the

Hispanic Society, yours is probably the only known example apart from the one in their possession. For that reason, it is worth a lot of money, particularly as it is not damaged. I cannot give you a price, but I am in touch with the Hispanic Society who will give me an approximate valuation once I have inspected your example.'

'It's not for sale,' said Father O'Hagan.

'Perhaps not, but it is a major asset for your church, should you ever be in need of funds, and for that reason it does need to be comprehensively insured for its market value, and re-valued regularly thereafter.'

'I don't know what to do. I'm disappointed it is not a relic of St Eulalia, but I accept your evaluation. I must admit I had my doubts, which I kept secret, even if the lady who left it to us was convinced of its provenance.'

'Well, there we are. We'll be in touch soon and I don't think the premiums will be too costly for the church, provided you keep the pot in a secure place.'

'I think St Eulalia has been looking after you very well indeed,' I said as we were leaving. 'She's given you something which is very useful from a financial security aspect, and there is a link between her and these pots, even if those links are a few centuries apart.'

'Well, yes, so if the church does need a lot of cash for a new roof or something else in an emergency, I could always ask her if we could sell her pot!'

'I'm not a Christian, Father,' said Mr Linden, 'but it does seem that someone is looking after you! And now we must be getting along. I am now going to examine an oil painting found in a farm barn . . . it might be a masterpiece, or it might be junk. Who knows?'

And so we left Father O'Hagan with his precious pot of ivory. I felt sure it would be on show next time the church celebrated St Eulalia's feast day. It might not contain olive oil or ashes or anything else, but I did wonder if it could be used as a flower vase. On her feast day? That was 10 December!

Six

'Today is Unemployment Sunday. Please remember in your prayers those who are seeking work and their families.'
                                    From a church notice board

Despite the inconvenience of my pot leg, I continued to hobble around the village on essential journeys such as my Wednesday morning trek up to the post office to pay in collected premiums, and across to the Unicorn for my market-day surgery. Evelyn came to the market too, some-times bringing Paul to see his grandparents even if they were busy, and there is no doubt our style of life was proving both useful and enjoyable. With each new Wednesday, it was evident that an increasing number of people expected me to be there during the afternoon – they came for advice or merely a chat, which is precisely as I had intended. As a consequence, I found myself always busy, recommending specific types of insurance to meet the individual needs of my diverse clients and even helping people to complete their claim forms, renewals or take out new policies. Attending to their needs at market had certainly reduced my travelling both in terms of time and expense, and from what my clients told me, the system suited them too. There might even be an argument for opening an office some-where, but I felt it would lack the atmosphere of this open air market. Besides, I wasn't a broker; I was an agent with a responsibility towards my many and varied policy holders. I would resist any suggestion from above that I should find an office!

On one occasion, I succeeded in selling a policy to a stall

holder who attended each week with shoes for sale. I discovered he owned a shop in Guisborough and that his premises and stock were comprehensively insured but his cover did not extend to the open-air market, and neither did it cover the journey to and from market. I pointed out that he put his valuable goods at risk every Wednesday – and those risks could come from a traffic accident, heavy rain and storms, theft and a host of other possible but unforeseen occurrences. Even though his busy shop was insured with a different company, he agreed to give me the business of insuring his weekly outing to, from and during the market. That was his way of thanking me – and that small success had arisen through nothing more than a casual chat during a lull in trading.

One of the regular customers at the market was Crocky Morris, with his ever-present basket of cups, plates and saucers. He did not have a stall, however, but traded from a heavy basket always balanced on his head, except when he was sitting down with a pint of ale before him. Only then would he place his basket on the floor. In his mid-seventies, he had traded in this manner for most of his life and even though his stomach was invariably full of beer, his speech slurred and his steps unsteady, Crocky was never known to have dropped his basket. Furthermore, in spite of his age he could out-run and out-balance any one who challenged him to a basket-carrying duel. Many had tried and failed; there was little doubt he was a living legend.

In the market outside the Unicorn, he would weave his way between the stalls, often being verbally rude to the stall holders and occasionally staggering dangerously close to delicate produce and goods, but never falling and never dropping his precious basket. I daren't even think what might happen if he did drop it and its contents among the cream and cheese, the glass and china or the fruit and vegetables.

In spite of the risks to himself and his wares, Crocky was one person who would not even consider taking out an insurance policy, either for himself or his load of crockery. Travelling on foot in all the villages in Delverdale, always with the basket balanced on his head and with visits to all the local pubs, even at 7 a.m. in some cases (thanks to generous landlords), he considered himself indestructible. Nonetheless, he was sometimes a liability. There were times when his unexpected appearances had startled motorists and horse-riders into having minor accidents which resulted in claims from their insurance policies. He would materialize unexpectedly and spectrelike from behind a tree or wall where he might have been relieving himself, or perhaps rise from a ditch on the roadside where he had lain down for a short nap, always with the full basket on his head. Even if the local people were not too fazed by his activities, visitors and tourists often found themselves worried or shocked by the scruffy apparition that suddenly confronted them with a massive basket on its head. Crocky was harmless, however, and would never hurt anyone, although his language could border on the insulting.

In spite of his strange way of life, Crocky himself seemed impervious to injury or accident and even when he left chaos in his wake, he escaped unscathed. Over the years, though, his antics had cost the Premier a considerable sum in successful claims from those he had inconvenienced, yet he had never claimed any insurance payments or compensation for himself. It was with the usual sense of trepidation, therefore, that I saw him emerge from the front door of the Unicorn in the middle of one Wednesday market-day afternoon.

He had been inside for a lengthy liquid dinner time, probably with a bag of crisps or a sandwich. That was his normal practice and I watched him hoist the heavy basket on to his head, execute a few wobbly steps backwards and forwards until he found his balance and then begin yet another tour of the stalls. I saw the looks of alarm cross the faces of the stall holders, all of them knowing that one day the inevitable would surely happen. In their minds, it was merely a question of time.

They thought it was a racing certainty that Crocky would one day stumble or trip and cast his heavy basket full of crockery into someone's precious display of wares. Today might well witness that occasion, but, as I waited, with more than a little apprehension, he managed to weave his precarious route through the stalls and the shoppers. The whole time, his basket was swaying as he negotiated sharp twists and turns to avoid collisions, with a few bends of his back to avoid crashing into any overhanging awning.

Then I saw him halt as a newcomer approached him. The man, whom I did not recognize, did not wish to buy one of Crocky's pots, however. It was evident he was asking directions and I saw Crocky point his finger in my direction. The man, who was smartly dressed with dark hair and probably in his mid-forties, then made his way towards me. Evelyn had just rejoined me, leaving Paul to go and collect some eggs from his granny's hen houses, and so we waited as the man headed our way.

'Mr Taylor?' he asked in a local accent. 'The insurance man?'

'Yes, that's me, and this is my wife, Evelyn.'

I was standing in front of the hole in the wall that contained my leaflets, proposal forms and a few business cards. I shook his hand, as did Evelyn, then I extracted a card and gave it to him.

He thanked me and said, 'I'm Alan Lyth. I run a photography business and camera shop in Guisborough. A small shop but it's a living. Weddings, baby and family photos, anniversaries, that sort of thing, they're my bread and butter. Lyth Photography, I call myself.'

'I can't say I know your shop,' I apologized. 'It's not often I get into Guisborough.'

'Well, we're always there if you need a professional family portrait, but I'm not here about my shop. It's about another project. I wondered if I might have a word?'

'Of course, that's why I am here. How can I help?'

'I've just been to a meeting with Mrs Pollard,' he began. I knew Mrs Pollard. In fact, everyone in the village knew Mrs Pollard. She was secretary of the parish council as well as the village hall committee, and was a member of umpteen different organizations in Micklesfield. 'She suggested I talk to you and that I'd find you here.'

As he spoke, I wondered which of her many hats Mrs Pollard had been wearing at the meeting. He went quickly into his subject, however.

'It's to do with the village hall,' he said. 'I've been talking to her about my plans to show films in the hall, a sort of small cinema. I possess my own projector and have access to all the latest productions. Already, I'm showing them at a hall in Guisborough each Friday evening, and I'm in discussions with the village hall committees in Lexingthorpe and Crossrigg to see whether a cinema is viable in those villages. I'd prefer to appear in Micklesfield because it's the largest village in the dale, hence my chat with Mrs Pollard, and you do have a particularly fine and spacious hall.'

'That would be wonderful!' Evelyn said. 'Films in our own village hall? At the moment we have to go all the way to Whitby if we want to go to the pictures; they've three cinemas so films must be popular. There's the Waterloo, the Empire and the Coliseum, all with ice-creams!'

'Well, I don't think I could run to selling ice-cream in the intervals but if someone in the village wanted to do so, then I'd not object. But it's not ice-cream I want to talk about, Mr Taylor.'

'Matthew,' I said. 'Most of my clients call me Matthew.'

'Mrs Pollard told me. Matthew's Insurance, she said.'

'I work for the Premier.' I felt I had to tell him I did not run my own company, and that neither was I a broker. 'So how can I help?'

'I need insurance for my shows,' he told me. 'Since electricity was installed in village halls like Micklesfield there's been concern about fire risks, but I need to have the necessary comprehensive cover for anything else that might harm the audience or damage the hall. The hall is insured in its own right, as indeed they all must be, and of course I have insurance for my equipment and the films I hire, but for specialist events in community halls there has to be extra cover for any additional risks.'

'That's no problem. We have other specialists on our books – dance tutors, the village orchestra and so forth – so we can easily find a policy to suit you.'

'You don't mind me coming to you about this, do you? I am insured through a Guisborough agent for my shop and photography business, but if I am working in a village, I like to give business to the local people. I find they appreciate that.'

'Like ice-cream sellers?'

'Like ice-cream sellers – and insurance agents!' He smiled.

'Of course I don't mind. And yes, the Premier can insure you. I'd need to know the frequency and duration of your shows, whether you will be charging for admission, whether food will be on sale during the intervals or before or after the show, the numbers expected to attend, whether the audience would include children and if so, whether there is any restriction on their ages, along with any other salient facts. I am sure you are aware of the rules governing the storage and use of cinematograph film too. I believe there is a considerable fire risk from celluloid film.'

'Yes, there is, but I know the regulations very well, and the safety requirements. I am aware of the kind of questions that need an answer on a proposal form too, as I've been through this exercise with other village halls and insurance companies, but at the moment this is just speculation. My plans are by no means complete. The village hall committee has yet to meet to decide whether or not to let me in! Their meeting's next week.'

'Doesn't the village hall need a licence from the council if films are to be shown to the public?'

'Yes, I'm aware of that; there are formalities to go through but they are not a problem. Once I get the go-ahead, then I'll contact you.'

'Fair enough, my card gives my home address and phone number and, thanks to this leg, I'll be at home for another few weeks. You can take a proposal form with you now and let me have it when you're ready to start.'

'Thanks. I think that's all we can do for now.'

'There is one other thing,' I said before he left. 'I'm putting together a village magazine, in fact I'm working on the first issue right now, and you're in time to beat the dead-line for adverts.'

I told him about the proposed content and circulation of the *Micklesfield Magazine,* and he seemed pleased because any publicity for him would be useful.

'I can wait a few more days,' I told him. 'If you'd like time to think about that, then I could include you. The magazine is really for Micklesfield only but I'm sure copies will find their way into other parts of the dale. It might draw in a few more customers for you.'

'Great! Right, that would be a good start!'

We parted amicably. News of his proposal would quickly spread around Micklesfield and indeed the rest of Delverdale, particularly as several market visitors and stall holders had overheard our conversation. I felt sure his plans would generate a very positive response, particularly among those who had been unable to travel into Whitby or Guisborough to see a film. When I returned home that after-noon, I checked in my own files for the special provisions and recommendations governing the insurance of places where cinematograph films were shown, and of the people who wished to show them to a paying audience. The rele-vant statute was the Cinematograph Act of 1909, along with various sets of regulations dating from 1923 to 1952, with the likelihood of the films catching fire being of constant official concern. Having done a modicum of research, I was confident that I – and the village hall – could cope with all of Mr Lyth's requirements.

Leaping ahead by a few months again, I have to say that the first double-feature film-show in Micklesfield village hall promised to be a delight. Instead of showing the most up-to-date films, Mr Lyth opted for a couple of firm favourites, one before the interval and the other afterwards. First was the all-time favourite and classic, *Shall We Dance,* in black and white, starring Fred Astaire and Ginger Rogers. It was scheduled to last for 101 minutes, followed by *Snow White and the Seven Dwarfs,* in colour; that would last for a further eighty minutes or so. It was a long programme but it attracted the crowds, old and young alike, including many who had already seen *Snow White* but couldn't resist a second viewing. Like most others in the village, Evelyn and I, along with baby Paul, decided to make a night of it and arrived early to be sure of securing good seats.

Even though we arrived almost three quarters of an hour before the start of the show, the place was filling rapidly, but we managed to obtain good seats with a clear view for young Paul. The huge white screen was standing on the stage, partially curtained before the show started; the stage curtains would be opened to reveal its full extent when Mr Lyth gave the word. The blinds of the hall and its thick window curtains were already closed to shut out the daylight and the lights were burning. The chairs were arranged in slightly curved rows with wide aisles to help everyone get a good view, and Roger Crossley from the shop had managed to secure an ice-cream handcart from a Whitby manufacturer. It would keep the ice-cream cool so that it could be sold at the interval. It meant we could all enjoy a cool ice-cream even if there would be a queue.

As the people were filing in and settling down, Mr Lyth was standing beside his projector at the back of the hall, just inside the main door. He was constantly testing the machine, running it backwards and forwards, spinning the spools, checking the focus and sound levels and generally ensuring everything was in fine working order. The projector was situated in the middle of the centre aisle, its leads trailing towards a power point at the back of the hall while other wires connected it to a pair of loud speakers, one at each side of the stage. A party atmosphere prevailed with everyone chattering excitedly as the minutes ticked towards the grand opening at seven o'clock.

Then it was time to start.

As the stage curtains were opened fully to reveal the screen, the interior lights were switched off and the hall was completely dark. The chatter stopped as the projector began to whirr noisily, then the screen was illuminated with a series of flickering numbers and letters before the title sequence began, together with the sound. I remember hoping the length of film wouldn't snap during the screening; that was something that often happened with this kind of projector, requiring urgent repairs to be made, often with sticky tape. Sometimes the sound went haywire too, or the pictures on the screen began to go backwards, or else they juddered as the film rode over the sprockets to distort the pictures and curdle the speech and music.

I hoped Mr Lyth was professional enough to have prepared and rehearsed his show in advance so that none of those all-too-regular accidents would mar his evening, or ours.

Things were going quite well for the first ten minutes or so as we watched a brief series of adverts before the film titles were shown and then, as the first main feature film was getting underway, the rear doors of the hall crashed open and light flooded into the hall. Someone had burst in and for a moment none of us had any idea what had happened – I thought it might be drunken youths being stupid, but there was only one figure, a man, and he carried a basket on his head. It was Crocky, with his basket of cups, saucers and plates. As the doors swung shut to restore the darkness, Crocky moved over the floor, making a considerable noise as he bumped into chairs at the back of the room.

Mr Lyth produced a hand-held torch to guide him to a seat, but he ignored it. He seemed to think that if he followed the beam of light that shone from the lens of the projector, it would guide him to a seat. He appeared to be heading for the front of the hall.

'Sit down, Crocky,' a man shouted. 'Sit on the floor if you can't find a seat! And put that basket down!'

'Yes, sit down!' shouted another man. 'And shut up!'

Crocky's reply is not fit to reproduce but in the meantime he had found his way towards the projector, just like a moth is attracted by light, and then he started to squeeze past it with the basket still on his head.

He managed to get past Mr Lyth and the whirring projector, clearly intent on gaining a front seat. Now, of course, the screen contained an enlarged silhouette of Crocky and his basket because he was moving within the width of the beam as it emerged from the projector. As he struggled against the bright light to see his way down the centre aisle, he tripped over one of the wires leading to a loudspeaker.

What happened next was a classic dance of the kind one might see in a Walt Disney cartoon, rather like an eight-legged insect dancing on hot coals as Crocky tried to maintain his balance and keep the basket on his head as he tripped and then hurtled down the aisle towards the stage. And all the time he was blinded by the brilliant light from the projector's lamp, blinking into it at times, turning his back upon it to try and regain his vision.

Whatever he did, it always seemed he had one leg desperately stamping ahead of the other as the heavy basket threatened to overbalance him. By some miracle, his old legs worked fast enough to maintain his balance and he reached a point on the floor which marked the centre point of the stage below the screen and then he promptly sat on the stage. It was low enough for him to do that. Still silhouetted on the screen, he removed the basket from his head and, blinking against the fierce light from the projector, carefully set it down at his side. At that point, everyone cheered.

Then the lights came up as Mr Lyth switched off his projector.

'Sit over there, Crocky!' It was Roger Crossley from the shop who was indicating a vacant chair. 'Leave your basket on the stage for now!'

'Can I have an ice-cream?'

'No you can't, they're for the interval.'

'Has it started?'

'Yes it has, and we're all trying to watch. Now, if you just sit down and keep quiet, you can enjoy it like the rest of us. All right, Mr Lyth, I think we can continue.'

'I'll start again; I wouldn't want us to think Crocky was trying to out-class Fred Astaire.'

'I can dance better than him,' said Crocky. 'Much lighter on my feet than he is, and he couldn't do it with a basket of pots on his head, like me.'

And so, with Crocky settled in a chair and his precious

basket of pots safe once more, we all settled down to watch Micklesfield's first film show.

It was an undoubted success and a very happy occasion, if a shade too long, although no-one seemed to mind having to sit through such a lengthy performance. But for months afterwards, people would only talk about Crocky's brief moment of fame, inevitably adding, 'Even though he tripped over the cables in the darkness and staggered the full length of the aisle, he didn't drop his basket.'

Memories of the community spirit which had prevailed throughout the Second World War were still strong in Micklesfield and the film show had revived some of that nostalgia.

There is little doubt that by bringing together people of every age and social background, the film show had revived the desire in many to enjoy similar events that would recapture the village wartime spirit. Venues would not be a problem – indoor functions could be held in the village hall, while the cricket field was always available for outdoor events. It was just a case of deciding upon something that appealed to everyone, and then finding a willing volunteer or two to arrange it.

It was the Wednesday following the first film show that I was again to be found at Micklesfield market. Mrs Jacqueline Pollard happened to be attending in the hope of buying some fresh fruit and vegetables and she stopped at my hole in the wall for a chat.

'I thought the film show was wonderful,' she oozed. 'Nice films, suitable for everyone's taste – and the chance to chat afterwards. It made me think the parish council should organize another social event for everyone. We need to regenerate some of that wartime camaraderie.'

'I agree; it's nice when the whole village gets together like that.'

'Have you any ideas, Matthew? You get around the villages and meet all sorts of people, so you must come across some ideas in your travels.'

'There is one I thought of,' I ventured, hoping I would

not be persuaded to take on the arrangements. 'It might bring everyone together.'

'Yes?'

'Well,' I said, 'when I was a child, I always had my Guy Fawkes bonfire night at home in the garden, with Dad letting off the fireworks and Mum baking potatoes and sausages in the fire. We had other kids around from nearby and some of my cousins came; they brought their own food and fireworks. It was a sort of jolly party even though it was November, very often cold and frosty. The fire was usually big enough and hot enough to keep us all warm, and on top of that, it was a wonderful way of getting rid of rubbish.'

'Me too, we always did that, and I did the same for my children. So what's your suggestion?'

'That the whole village gets together over a giant bonfire. Everyone could give something to burn, which would not be problem. I would think some would regard it as a wonderful way of getting rid of junk. The fireworks could be pooled with teams of adults to set them off, and each family could bring enough food for themselves. There would have to be some kind of organization and control, with an emphasis on safety, particularly with children around, but it would mean everyone could get together in a party atmosphere.'

'Hmm,' she muttered. 'You could have a point. We do have rather a lot of separate bonfires around the village on Guy Fawkes night, don't we? We have fireworks going off all over the place, frightening cats and dogs and terrifying the old folks who think the war has started all over again, and wondering if it's an air raid.'

'Children can let them off irresponsibly too, so a communal bonfire would hopefully reduce that.'

'It would indeed. So if everyone went to one location – say the cricket field – then it would mean just one fire and just one session of letting off those bangers and rockets. And the cricket field is far enough away for the bangs not to alarm old folks and animals.'

'Exactly,' I said.

'All right, Matthew, I think this is a good idea. It is your idea, so do you mind if I bring it up at the next council meeting?'

'Not at all, but I think the council should be responsible for the arrangements, if it is to be a village effort.'

'Yes, of course, I wouldn't want to press you into taking that on, not with you being such a busy man already. All right, Matthew, leave it with me and I'll let you know how things develop.'

After testing the idea on several key residents of Micklesfield, the parish council decided to go ahead and formed a small sub-committee to make the arrangements. Almost immediately, however, they encountered a problem – the cricket club would not permit a huge bonfire to be lit on the cricket field, even though the parish council promised it would not be established anywhere near the pitch. It would be somewhere in the outfield, where there was sufficient space, but the club was adamant – in addition to the problems of a fire anywhere near the pitch, there was the inevitable risk of fire to the pavilion and changing rooms. Rockets might land anywhere!

Furthermore, November could be a wet month and lots of feet paddling around the muddy wet field could cause immense damage to both the pitch and outfield. With great reluctance, therefore, the cricket club felt it necessary to refuse permission – after all, Micklesfield's cricket pitch was the finest in Delverdale and it had to be maintained in perfect condition.

I was attending my usual hole-in-the-wall stint on market day when Mrs Pollard came to break the bad news.

'I'm sorry, Matthew. The council thought a communal bonfire was a wonderful idea but we must take account of the concerns of the cricket club.'

'There must be a suitable field somewhere around the village, somewhere out of the way where the noise wouldn't alarm animals and people.'

'There are plenty of fields in and around the village,' she said. 'We've explored the idea of using one or two, but they belong to farms, with animals nearby, and none of the owners fancy a bonfire with kids and fireworks on their premises.'

It was while we were discussing the problem that Big Deck emerged from the pub wanting a break from the smoky atmosphere in the bar. The smoke was often as dense as a moorland fog. It stained the walls and ceilings and left a powerful smell that clung to the curtains as well as the clothing and hair of the customers.

'You two look serious!' he chortled. 'You look as if you've lost a fiver and found sixpence!'

I explained what had happened and he nodded in agreement with the cricket's club's decision, and with the reasoning of local farmers.

'Aye, I can see their reasoning. So far as the club is concerned, that pitch is the pride of the dale, we mustn't make a mess of it,' he grunted, then added, 'Why don't you take the fire up to the beacon? They've had fires on Micklesfield Beacon for centuries, to warn us about the Spanish Armada and other invasions and plagues . . . It's t'ideal place for a big bonfire. Bags of space, nowt to be damaged. It's a bit out of the village but mebbe that's a good thing if folks are likely to be scared by all the bangs and rockets going off. You can't do much harm up there.'

'Ah, yes, I know it,' said Mrs Pollard. 'I've never been up there; isn't it somewhere behind the top of Hollowood Hill?'

'That's the one, it's a big open space, no-one knows who owns it for sure; it's common land. There's a green lane running past it, back into the dale behind the hill. Horses and carts would use it but not cars, not since they made a proper road up there.'

'If it's common land, the parish council will be responsible for it,' said Mrs Pollard. 'I'm surprised I have not seen references in the council minutes.'

'It's not in Micklesfield parish,' Deck told us. 'It's just over the boundary, in Graindale Bridge parish.'

'Then I'll have words with Ted Cleghorn from Graindale – he's their parish council chairman – just to be on the safe side.'

When Mrs Pollard spoke to Ted Cleghorn he was full of enthusiasm and thought the bonfire was a wonderful idea, so much so that he asked if the villagers of Graindale and district could join in. He agreed that the old beacon was the perfect venue, adding that he thought the last time it had featured a beacon fire was when a rumour spread around the dale that Napoleon was going to invade. In our case, the fire would probably be larger than any which had served as beacons, and an additional factor was that fireworks would be involved. There were laws about the use of fireworks – for example, one law said it was illegal to set fireworks off in a street, but that wouldn't apply to the beacon.

Another regulation made it unlawful to light fires or throw any fireworks within fifty feet of the centre of the highway, and once more, the beacon was far enough away from the road for that not to be a problem. The police also had the power to confiscate any firework that did not conform to the safety rules, although some were not rigidly controlled from the safety aspect, such as sparklers, those weighing less than an eighth of an ounce, jumping crackers and others that were known as throwdowns. For this reason, and because Mrs Pollard did not want any kind of trouble at the bonfire, she decided that our village policeman, PC Clifford, would be informed and asked to attend in his uniform. He would advise on any likely breaches of the law or safety regulations.

Inevitably the question of insurance arose, but Mrs Pollard reminded us that the legitimate activities of parish councils were covered by the county council's all-embracing policy. The only proviso was that the county council's legal department was officially made aware of the event. It meant there was no need for my professional involvement, although I did make a mental note to include a reference to the bonfire in a suitable future issue of the *Micklesfield Magazine*.

As is always the case with this kind of communal event, the excitement began to rise as the great day approached, with people clearing rubbish from their attics and outbuildings, preparing food and buying fireworks. Even at that early stage, it was evident the community spirit remained strong as everyone did something towards making the night happy and successful. The parish council sub-committee had done a good job in publicizing the event and securing volunteers to supervise the fire, let off the fireworks and generally keep an eye on the proceedings. PC Clifford promised to attend as an additional method of persuading some of the more wayward youths to behave themselves and not spoil things for others, and soon everyone was looking forward to Bonfire Night. Even if the weather created a typical November evening of fog, frost or even snow, it would not spoil the occasion.

Lighting-up time was 6.30 p.m. with the first fireworks being let off at 7 p.m.; supper would be served from 7.30 p.m. and the party was expected to end around 9.30 p.m. Trestle tables were erected for the spread and everyone who brought food was asked to place it on the tables, along with any drinks. Big Deck had donated two barrels of beer, which proved very popular, while Mrs Curtis had made dozens of her famous rock buns.

It is difficult to estimate numbers but I tried to do a quick count, if only out of curiosity, and reckoned there were around three hundred people, many of them small children and teenagers. Among the faces in the glow of the flames I could see people from all age groups, some of whom I recognized but lots of strangers too. Then I noticed Crocky Morris moving steadily among the crowd, inevitably with his basket on his head. I wondered if he ever took it off, except when drinking beer. Even when attending this kind of social event, Crocky always carried his famous basket – I suppose it was like someone wearing a favourite cap and never appearing in public without it.

Evelyn and I had gone along with baby Paul, who was mesmerized by the sheer scale of the fire, and when the fireworks began to crackle and explode all around, with rockets colouring the sky high above the glow of the blaze, we thought he would be nervous. But he was jumping up and down and shouting with joy as the colourful scene unfolded around him. As the evening moved towards its inevitable conclusion with a co-ordinated display of extra-special fireworks organized by the volunteers, so the fire began to die down, the food and drink was exhausted and it was time for us all to go home. It had been a wonderful evening with no trouble from boisterous youngsters and the fact that two villages had joined forces added an extra dimension which included the renewal of former friendships. I could hear people around me saying how much they had enjoyed the evening and that they hoped it would be held next year, and the year after that, *ad infinitum*.

Evelyn and I left at nine o'clock because Paul was ready for bed and we had a long walk home, almost a mile in fact. We were not alone. Most of the revellers were leaving at the same time and so the long walk in the chill, dark November evening air became yet another example of friendliness and camaraderie.

I think the procession of walkers numbered about 100, or even 120; some were singing their favourite war songs such as Vera Lynn's 'We'll Meet Again' and 'It's a long way to Tipperary' while others chattered happily.

But then, as we were steadily making our way down the steep incline of Hollowood Hill towards Micklesfield railway station, there was a commotion towards the rear. I heard someone start to shout loudly in language that threatened to turn the night air blue and then came the sound of running feet amid the crackle of fireworks. As I was taller than most, I could look over their heads and saw the spectacle of Crocky Morris running as if all the hounds in hell were chasing him. Somebody, so it seemed, had dropped a few jumping jacks and small bangers into his basket, and now they were igniting . . . I had no idea whether a fuse was connecting them or whether they had been part of the final display that had been purloined, or whether one firework was setting off the others. But whatever the cause of the display, it was spectacular if harmless.

We were all treated to the sight of Crocky galloping to escape from the bangs and flashes, perhaps thinking the crackers had been fastened to his coat tail. Of course, he daren't lift the basket from his head in case he put his hand on to a live firework, and so he ran. I don't know why he ran because he could not escape from the fireworks unless

he stopped, took off his basket and removed the problem
– but that might have been slightly dangerous. He might
have burned himself.

Running must have seemed the best option for Crocky.
Everyone cheered as he hurtled past us and the last sight
of that memorable evening was of Crocky Morris, basket
on his head, running down Hollowood Hill with his pots
alive to the lights and sounds of firecrackers.

And still the basket never fell from his head.

Seven

'The Slimmers Club will meet at 7 p.m. on Thursdays in the Methodist Hall. Please use the large double doors at the side entrance.'

From a parish notice board

When any of my clients died, it was never easy deciding when to visit the family to discuss insurance matters. At such a delicate and emotional time, there never was an ideal opportunity – one could be much too early or much too late, and inevitably there was a feeling that one was intruding upon the grief. As representative of the Premier Assurance Association, however, I had responsibilities both to my company and to the client's surviving relatives, and at times it was necessary to put emotion and sensitivities to one side so that essential work could be done. Inevitably after a death there were necessary formalities and legal procedures to be followed, often in consultation with the family solicitor or with the executors of any will. It was my job to ensure the insured person's affairs were concluded as quickly and efficiently as possible, albeit with decorum. In some cases, the family urgently required cash from a life policy so that funeral expenses, or indeed other bills, could be met. Of course, if the deceased was the family breadwinner, then money from an insurance policy could be vital in maintaining solvency for the survivors, if only until the estate had been finalized. In most cases when a death occurred, the family would contact me rather than wait for me to contact them, and that eliminated those inevitable moments of anxiety in me.

Almost without exception, bereaved families wanted any outstanding matters of insurance to be settled as quickly and as smoothly as possible Unfortunately there were occasions, albeit rare, when I was unaware that a local person had died. That might occur if the death had been very sudden or unexpected, or if I was away from home. But if a person died after a long illness or perhaps due to a serious traffic accident, then in most cases I would probably become aware of it very quickly. I could even anticipate the deaths of some ailing people simply by talking to families and other villagers during my rounds and in some cases I could quietly begin the necessary arrangements to deal with their affairs. Even so, there were times I learned of a death as the funeral was being arranged or even, occasionally, some time afterwards.

News of a death was still passed around the moorland villages chiefly by word of mouth because few of the residents had telephones, and neither could they afford to place an advertisement in the local newspaper. Furthermore, not everyone took a newspaper – there were people who had never read a word since leaving school at the age of fourteen. An added factor was that moorland funerals were seldom large or splendid affairs. Usually they were very modest and very solemn, with cost being a vital factor, and even as late as the 1950s mourners were sometimes 'bidden' to attend. This was a very old Yorkshire rural custom that survived in a few isolated moorland areas, although it had ceased in the towns and larger villages.

To be bidden meant receiving an invitation – not by a letter or telephone call, but in person because the bidder, usually a parish church official, went around the dale knocking on selected doors to issue an invitation to both the church service and the funeral tea. It was considered extremely rude not to attend even though there were times when a bidden person was not closely acquainted with the deceased. I knew of one elderly gentleman who was holidaying in a moorland village when he was bidden to attend a local funeral. He pointed out that he was merely on holiday and did not know the deceased, but the bidder said, 'You've been bidden, therefore you must attend.' And so he did.

In the more remote corners of my agency, bidding to funerals was still practised and I was sometimes bidden to attend those of people who were not my clients. This invitation also meant partaking of the ham tea that followed, but if one of my clients did pass away in a remote community, I always made a point of attending the service in church or chapel even if I had not been bidden. That was quite acceptable – anyone was welcome to attend the service and indeed the funeral tea but those who had been bidden were *expected* to attend. Sometimes when I had not been bidden to the funeral, I did not partake of the ham tea, for I regarded that aspect of funerals as secondary to the religious send-off. Today, the bidding custom is no longer practised – but funeral teas consisting of ham are still very popular!

Ham was perhaps the ultimate sign of status at a moors funeral. Most widows, however poor, would want to boast that she had buried her husband 'wi' 'am'. If the relatives could say the deceased had been buried 'with ham' it was a sign of the standing of the family rather than their wealth. Not surprisingly, a funeral tea with ham was considered one of the finest send-offs anyone could have, although a cortège with black horses and a black horse-drawn hearse was also mightily effective. This emulated the Victorian custom of making funerals rather grand and very socially important occasions, so the dales people would do their best for the deceased, even on an extremely modest budget. I can recall funeral processions passing through moorland villages on their way to the church, when all the curtains along the route would be closed, and everyone in the street would stand still until the cortège had passed, with men removing their hats or saluting the coffin.

The funeral would be followed by a suitable period of mourning, with the widow or widower wearing black for up to three months afterwards – longer in some cases. People in mourning did not attend public events or happy social occasions either – men wouldn't pop into the local pub for a pint or two, nor would anyone attend things like parties, theatres or cinemas. Even weddings were not favoured during that period. This visual display of how much the dear departed was remembered, loved and missed began to wither after the First World War, and by the end of the Second World War the custom had virtually disappeared from our social lives.

There is no doubt the two wars resulted in the abandonment of many funeral traditions, even in remote areas of Britain, but it took a long time for the Victorian attitude towards death and funerals to completely fade from our moorland way of life.

In my capacity as editor of the *Micklesfield Magazine*, I had to remain alert to all local births, deaths and marriages because, almost without exception, families wanted such announcements to be included in any local publication, often at very short notice. In cases of death, they also liked a small obituary or tribute of some kind, but this was not always possible due to a lack of space. However, in my capacity as the Premier's local agent, I had to be constantly aware of the deaths of my clients. At times, it meant checking in my records to see whether a recently deceased person did hold a life policy – some had been arranged long before my appointment as the Delverdale agent, with the clients paying their premiums by cheque, usually quarterly and direct to Head Office. That meant there was no reason for me to pay regular visits, although if they lived within my agency, their names were in my records. In addition, there were occasions where a man had taken out a life policy with my company, but had failed to inform his wife or family of his action. I think that came about because, when money was in short supply (as it usually was in rural areas), many wives and families felt that spending hard-earned housekeeping funds on something intangible like an insurance policy was tantamount to throwing it away or even gambling.

In their carefully organized lives, money was for spending on essentials such as the house, food and clothes, not frivolous things like insurance speculations. Some men, and indeed some women, therefore adopted secrecy when negotiating their policies, but this could produce complications.

One example was the case of Ronald Newby, a retired carpenter who lived with his wife, Olive, in a cottage called Beckside at Crossrigg. On the riverside, not far from the railway station, the cottage was owned by the local brickworks; Ronald had spent most of his working life there, being responsible for the maintenance of the timberwork in its many buildings. The cottage was rented to him at a very small cost and he also had a tiny works pension but, like so many people in retirement, he relied heavily upon his life savings. There were also the formidable housekeeping skills of his wife who could make £1. 0s.0d. stretch as far as most people would stretch £10. 0s.0d. Beyond doubt, Ronald and Olive lived a very modest life, with an occasional drink at the pub as Ronald's one luxury, but he would carry out small carpentry jobs for others and this earned him a little extra pocket money. In his back yard there was a small outbuilding that he had converted into a workshop and the general impression was that Ronald and Olive, both in their late sixties, were very content in their retirement. But Ronald had a secret. Unknown to Olive, he had taken out an endowment assurance policy in his name, and it would mature when he reached his seventieth birthday.

If he died before reaching that birthday, then the monies would be paid to his estate, which meant Olive would receive them. If she died before him, then the monies would go to his two sons and one daughter. This was Ronald's way of preparing for the future and of leaving something worthwhile for his descendants, but he did not inform Olive because she would be angry with him for spending so much money on what she regarded as a form of gambling.

The policy was a large one, with high premiums, but upon maturity on his seventieth birthday, it would produce £2,500, a large sum when an annual salary for a working man was in the region of £250 or £300. There is no doubt

Olive would have welcomed, as part of her limited house-keeping budget, the extra money he spent on premiums and, had she known of the plan, she would have been very angry and upset at what she regarded as a waste of good money. To maintain the secrecy, Ronald had made arrange-ments for the premiums to be paid in cash without Olive knowing about them. Every month, he left money with a neighbour who was also his closest friend. This arrange-ment had been agreed long before I became the Premier's Delverdale agent but when I took over the area I was happy to continue this well-meant deceit. Each month, therefore, I would visit the neighbour, whose name was Harry Bentley, collect the cash and record the payment in my collecting book.

Most of the premiums came from Ronald's spare-time carpentry work and it was to be his surprise for Olive when he reached seventy – his earnest desire was that both could then live in happiness and financial security for the rest of their lives. They'd also be able to pay their funeral expenses. To explain the disappearance of his extra income, he told Olive he was saving up for a rainy day, and would rattle his large cash box which contained a lot of loose chance and some notes. He could explain some expendi-ture by saying he needed regular supplies of glue, wood, nails and screws for his carpentry, and sometimes the replacement or purchase of important tools. He said his few drinks at the pub came out of that cash. His minor web of deceit appeared to convince her.

One reason for taking out this large policy was that longevity ran in both his family and that of his wife. His own parents and grandparents had lived into their eighties, and so had Olive's, and consequently there was every chance he and she would do likewise. A long life would enable him to produce a magnificent sum of invested cash and then survive for several more years to enjoy it.

But nature has a habit of confounding the best laid plans. One morning before his seventieth birthday, Ronald collapsed and died in his workshop. He was sixty-eight. For a week or so afterwards, I was completely unaware of this because Evelyn was doing my collecting and no-one had thought to tell her. After all, Olive Newby had no idea her husband was insured with the Premier.

Furthermore, Ronald's fellow conspirator, Harry Bentley, happened to be spending a week's holiday with his brother and his wife in the Lake District, so he was unable to alert me to Ronald's unexpected end.

It would be eight or nine days afterwards that someone knocked on my door just as I was preparing a cup of tea and a jam tart for my morning break. As usual, Evelyn was collecting in the dale, Paul was with Aunt Maureen and I was working on the *Micklesfield Magazine*, preparing a page layout to cope with an unexpected influx of adverts. Now there was no doubt I'd need twelve pages. When I went to answer the knock, I found our village policeman, PC Clifford, standing there.

'Morning, Matthew,' he smiled. 'Have I caught you at a bad time?'

'No, not at all. In fact, I'm making a pot of tea and have found some jam tarts in the pantry. Have you time to join me?'

'I never say no to a jam tart and a cup of tea,' he smiled, removing his peaked cap and following me into the house. I led him into the kitchen and instead of using my office we sat at the table as the kettle sang its way towards boiling. He plonked his cap on the table and I placed the jam tarts on a plate, organized a milk jug and some sugar and made the tea. Then I settled down to join him.

'So what can I do for you, Ted?'

He was a stolid constable, always smartly turned out, with neat black hair and a carefully trimmed black moustache. In his mid-forties, he had been Micklesfield's village bobby for about ten years and seemed settled here, with no thoughts of promotion or of moving to another station. He was a good policeman, respected and admired by the villagers. His beat covered several Delverdale villages and hamlets and he had a small motor scooter to transport him around his large and hilly patch.

'It's about Ron Newby,' he began.

'Ron?' I had not heard anything about Ronald. 'What's happened?'

'You've not heard? Oh dear, well, this is bad news. Sorry to break it like this. He was found dead in his workshop last week.'

'Oh dear, poor Olive . . . what a shock.'

'Aye, it must have been, but I've got to prepare a sudden death report for the coroner. Form 48 has to be completed.' He pulled a buff envelope from his tunic pocket and extracted the necessary foolscap form. It contained a lot of questions with spaces for the answers. 'I've got to ask you a few questions,' he continued as he spread the form on the table and took out a fountain pen.

'Me? Why do you want to ask me questions about Ron Newby?'

'It's about his life insurance,' he said almost conspiratorially. 'I had words with his wife and she told me he wasn't insured; it's one of the questions on Form 48. But I've heard a whisper that he *was* insured. I have to state whether or not his life was insured and, if so, for how much and by which company. The coroner has to be notified.'

I knew those questions formed part of all enquiries into sudden and unexplained deaths and, if there was an inquest, those facts could form part of the evidence presented to the coroner. If a post-mortem was held, it would identify the cause of death and if it was found to be due to natural causes, then there would be no inquest. It was the task of the police to enquire into all aspects of the death and if any suspicious circumstances were revealed, then subsequent enquiries might involve CID, inevitably with a coroner's inquest. The fact that a deceased person was heavily insured, with someone else benefiting from his or her death, was seen by some as a possible motive for murder. But surely this was not the case with Ronald Newby?

'So is there a problem?' I asked before providing an answer to his question.

'Let's say things are not straightforward, Matthew. The

post-mortem revealed an injury to Ron's head, at the back. It was enough to break the skin but not the skull. Quite a nasty knock though. And when he was found, there was a heavy wooden mallet lying beside his body.'

'So who found him?'

'The postman, who often arrived when Ron was in his workshop.'

'So was that the cause of death?' I asked.

'No, he died from heart failure but the pathologist drew our attention to the head wound and suggested we make further enquiries so that the coroner is fully informed. We need to explain the presence of the mallet and the blow to his head. We've had the Scenes of Crime Officers there photographing the workshop, testing for fingerprints and so forth, but there is also the vexed question of the insurance. Mrs Newby insists her husband's life was not insured, Matthew. I've learned that that is not true. I spoke to a neighbour, Harry Bentley, who was away in the Lake District when it happened and he said Ron was heavily insured with a life policy. Through you.'

'Yes, he was,' I said, and I explained that it was an endowment assurance due to mature when Ron reached seventy years of age; if he died before reaching that age, then the policy would be paid in full to his dependants, and I told PC Clifford that the sum due would be £2,500 with profits.

'A lot of money for a family like the Newbys, Matthew. So what amount of profits will be added? How much are we talking about?'

'I don't know the exact amount. The policy has been running for some years so they will be quite substantial – somewhere between £250 and £300 at a rough guess, but possibly more.'

'So Olive Newby is set for a massive windfall, eh? No wonder she denies knowing about the insurance.'

'Good grief, Ted, you're not suggesting she's responsible, are you?'

'Stranger things have happened, Matthew. After years of struggling to cope, folks get to the end of their tether,

can't face the future, something snaps and bingo! They
go berserk. We never know what goes on behind closed
doors, even in the nicest of households. And remember
he was hit on the head, probably by that mallet. A shock
of that kind could result in a heart attack . . .'

'But she's telling the truth, Ted. She had no idea Ronald
was insured; he didn't tell her. She hated the idea of risking
her hard-earned cash on what she regarded as gambling.
She needed all the cash she could get hold of just to keep
the household running. On Ron's income and then his
pension, there was nothing spare for things like gambling
or speculation, as she saw it. Ronald earned a bit extra
with his carpentry work and took out a big policy, in secret,
so he and Olive would be comfortable in their final years.
He paid the premium out of his spare-time carpentry earn-
ings. It was his way of saving for the future. Harry handed
the premiums to me so Olive would never know.'

'Hmm. I'm pleased to hear that, it confirms what Harry
Bentley, told me but it still doesn't explain that knock on
the head.'

'I can't answer that, Ted, but I didn't initiate the policy.
It was done before I took over this agency, but you could
have words with my predecessor, Jim Villiers. I think he
negotiated it with Ronald and helped to devise that secret
method of paying the premiums so Olive would never
know. He'll support what you've been told.'

'I know where Jim lives, thanks for the tip. The more
confirmation I can rustle up, the better it looks for Olive.'

'There is another point, Ted. Even if Olive suspected
he was putting a bit aside for an insurance policy, she
would never know how much it was worth on maturity,
unless she asked me. And she's never done that.'

'A good point, but even that still doesn't explain the
knock on the head.'

PC Clifford's task was to answer the questions on his
Form 48 so that the coroner's report could be completed,
but the question of whether this was a murder case would
not rest with him. The CID would carry out the necessary
investigation with help from forensic scientists. When PC

Clifford left, I was in a quandary because I felt absolutely certain that Olive Newby would never do any harm to her husband. It was simply not in her nature . . . Or was it?

It would be a couple of weeks later before PC Clifford returned, this time looking much happier about his visit. Once more over tea and jam tarts, he felt he should inform me about the outcome of the police enquiries.

'As we said earlier, Matthew, death was from natural causes, a heart attack in simple terms. When we studied the workshop, the photographs of the body as it had fallen, the location of Ron's tools and lengths of timber stored in his workshop, along with a very intense interview with his wife, plus the scientific input, it became clear it was nothing more than a natural death. Ron, who was alone at the time, had had a seizure and as he had fallen he had grabbed at the first thing he could hope to catch hold of – it happened to be a plank of wood standing beside his work bench. That had fallen with him and in doing so had knocked the mallet from its hooks – it hung there on the wall like a hammer might – and as it fell, it hit Ron on the head. It didn't cause his death – if the poor chap had lived, it might have given him a headache or a nasty cut but no more. Certainly not enough to kill him, and the pathologist doesn't think it would have caused a heart attack. Poor old Ron was probably dead before he grabbed that piece of wood; the pathologist thinks he was dead before he hit the ground. After what we learned from you and the others about the insurance, the coroner does not want an inquest. He has issued the necessary burial certificate, so the funeral can go ahead.'

'So Olive now has a nice nest egg?'

'She says she can now afford to buy Ronald the finest tombstone ever seen in Crossrigg churchyard, with space for her name when she joins him. And plenty of flowers all through the years.'

'Does she know she was suspected of murder, if only for a very short time?' I felt I had to ask.

'No, we took care never to give her that impression.'

'Ronald would have been horrified, wouldn't he? The

thought that his generous act all those years ago could have led to his lovely wife being suspected of killing him.'

'I don't think any of the police really thought she had done it,' smiled PC Clifford. 'But it does show how totally innocent actions can lead to some unwelcome conclusions!'

'So never cheat on your wife and family!' I said. 'That's the message in this case!'

'Is there a husband or wife anywhere who has never, ever cheated, even just a little, on his or her other half? Even just a teeny-weeny white lie?' Ted Clifford rose to leave. 'If there is, I'd like to meet him or her.'

There was another occasion when secrecy in a family's insurance dealings caused distress to a farmer, although it did not involve a death or a funeral. Joe Webster and his wife Jane were sheep farmers whose isolated premises comprised a windswept spread on the upper slopes of Baysthorpe Dale Head. Upon the North York Moors, the top of a dale (i.e. where a stream or river is likely to begin) is known as the dale head, and the place where it opens on to a plain, often with a village located there, is known as the end. Thus dale head and dale end can be several miles apart.

Joe and Jane had two children, both boys of primary-school age, and they attended Baysthorpe primary school at dale end. The Websters were successful because they worked extremely hard, at times in ferocious weather, when both could be seen on the heights tending their flock of black-faced moorland sheep. At lambing time, they worked day and night to ensure the ewes and their new offspring were cared for.

Instead of hiring extra labour for special tasks they would clip the wool of their own sheep and dip them to prevent disease in accordance with the regulations. It was non-stop tough work, but both Joe and Jane enjoyed their isolated and busy existence, with their two little boys old enough to help on occasions. Certainly, the youngsters enjoyed looking after newborn lambs, helping with the dipping and collecting the eggs from their few head of poultry. It was a family enterprise that served as a model to others.

Joe, tall, blond, red-cheeked, sturdy and handsome in a weathered sort of way, was a familiar figure at sheep sales and livestock markets, always seeking to secure the best possible deal. A knowledgeable and experienced sheep farmer, he drove a rather battered Land Rover and trailer but believed his tough, remote farmstead was no place for smart new vehicles and machinery. If his wife wanted to drive into town for any reason, then she had to tolerate his scruffy old vehicle. In spite of its rough location, the premises and outbuildings were always tidy and well-maintained, whilst the interior of the farmhouse was clean, comfortable and cosy, a necessity in winter upon its lonely site. Jane, with her dark brown hair worn long but generally clad in some kind of rough all-embracing apron, was practical but tough too. When she dressed up to attend a function in the village or to go to town, however, she emerged as a beautiful and elegant young woman, the pride of any man.

The difference in her appearance when she was away from the farm was nothing short of astonishing. Everyone who knew them said they were a lovely, friendly and devoted couple, an example to others and as trustworthy as anyone could be. From my point of view, however, there was a major problem – they were insured with the National Farmers' Union, one of the most prevalent competitors in my rural agency. Much as I would have liked to secure their business with the Premier, it was my personal decision never to attempt to poach any clients from other agents or companies who operated within my agency. If someone wished voluntarily to transfer their business to me, then I was quite happy to accept it, but I felt that deliberately targeting and pressuring the customers of another insurance company was morally wrong.

The fact that the Websters were clients of the NFU meant I never visited their farm on insurance business. I had been a couple of times to look at motorbikes that Joe had advertised for sale, and I had encountered both Joe and Jane in Baysthorpe on several occasions when they had come down to the village. Although I knew them by sight and was on speaking terms with both, I could not claim their friendship or a customer relationship.

It was with considerable surprise, therefore, that I responded to a knock on my back door one afternoon when I was still at home with my leg in plaster. Joe Webster was outside, having driven into Micklesfield in his old Land Rover.

I responded quickly enough not to show my real surprise, and invited him inside. I led him through to my office and offered him a cup of tea, but he refused, saying he couldn't stay very long as he had to pick the children up from school. He noticed my pot leg and offered his sympathies, saying it had once happened to him when he was playing football for the village team. He knew just how inconvenient a broken leg could be, especially in his profession.

'So how can I help you?' I asked when he was settled.

'I'm a bit cautious about asking you a favour, Matthew, seeing I've got my farm and all that goes with it insured with the NFU, but I think the time has come for me to ask.'

'Well, if I can help, I will. If I know what you want, I'll give you an honest answer.'

I could see he was having difficulty expressing his precise wishes and I detected a slight show of emotion in his voice. Yorkshire moorland farmers are not known for being emotional unless a favourite cow, horse, pig or sheep dies, but this seasoned and tough farmer was definitely upset about something. I waited for him to gather whatever courage was necessary.

'I'd like to leave the NFU.' He spoke as if he'd had tremendous difficulty finding the words. 'Can I do that? I mean, can I come over to Matthew's Insurance after being with the NFU all my working life, and my dad before me? The farm and its outbuildings, the vehicles, machinery, some of the livestock, the house and domestic contents . . . the lot in fact.'

'Well, the short answer is yes. It's no problem. I could easily arrange a transfer to the Premier, but with a farm the size of yours I might need to bring one of my bosses to discuss things with you, and we'd also need an assessment of its current value. Total value that is, to include everything you want adding to the policy – animals, vehicles, machinery, buildings, the lot. The chap who comes will probably be my District Ordinary Branch Sales Manager; he's called Wilkins and I'm sure he'd bring one of our expert assessors. We'd need a professional assessment to decide the amount of cover required, and that would also affect your premiums. In such cases, we always honour any no-claims bonuses you have accrued over the years, and I like to think our premiums would be lower than the NFU, but our cover would be as good if not better.'

'Sounds all right by me,' he said.

'So do you want me to go ahead and start the ball rolling?'

'Aye,' he said shortly.

'So does the farm belong to you? It's not owned by an estate or other organization?'

'No, it's all mine, Matthew, lock, stock and barrel. Well, I say mine, but in fact we're in partnership – me and Jane, my wife. Equal partners. My dad wasn't like that; Mum owned nowt but a few hens. But we're different. I believe in wives sharing everything.'

'That's a forward way of looking at things!'

'Well, she puts just as much effort into it as I do. We do own the lot, and there's no mortgage. It was handed down to me and I'll hand it on to my lads one of these days. Been in the family for more than two hundred years, allus with sheep. You'd never get crops to grow on those moors and there's no grassland to sustain cattle, so we've never tried. Just sheep and a few head of poultry and geese.'

'So when do you want to me start arranging the transfer?'

'Just as soon as you like, Matthew.'

'These things do take a little time due to the considerations we have to bear in mind and the formalities involved. The first thing I must do is have words with Mr Wilkins, who's based at our District Office at Ryethorpe. It's a case of making an appointment for him and one of our specialists to make an assessment of everything on your farm and in the house.'

'Aye, that's to be expected.'

'Once it has been duly assessed, we would seek your agreement to our valuation – you could always get an independent valuer to confirm our figures. Then if we all agree, the company would make a formal written offer, to include everything that you need us to cover, hopefully comprehensively, and then we would complete a proposal form, just for the file.'

'I'm not one for much paperwork, but I know you'll help me.'

'I'll do all I can to help, Joe. Now, acceptance of the transfer normally takes a few days and our company will notify the NFU to make sure all their records are transferred to us, and then cancelled in their files. We're probably talking about a week or two at the most.'

'Right, well, all I can say is get cracking, Matthew. The sooner the better so far as I'm concerned.'

'Can I ask one thing? Clearly, my bosses will want to know what has prompted you to seek a transfer from the NFU. Are you prepared to tell me?'

'I'll tell you, Matthew, because you're a local lad and to be trusted, and because everyone I've talked to says you are the most honest and decent insurance man they've ever come across. But I wouldn't want you to tell your bosses. Just tell them it's because I think the Premier's better than the NFU.'

'I don't want to pry, Joe. If it's some very personal reason, then perhaps it's best kept to yourself.' It sounded to me as if he'd had some kind of unhappy experience with the NFU, some personal matter that had led to this decision, but there was no reason why I should know that. As he said, he wanted to transfer his business to me simply because the Premier offered the best cover and best terms.

'Nay, you asked so I'm going to tell you, so long as it never gets beyond these four walls. If you're going to be my insurance man and adviser, you need to know these things.'

'Well, I won't press you.'

'And that's why I'm going to tell you, Matthew. It's because that NFU chap is paying too much attention to my wife. That's why. I'm not saying she's been unfaithful or owt like that, or that she ever would be, but she's my wife, the mother of my bairns and my partner in business, so the best way to nip it in the bud is to stop him calling at the farm. Give him no reason to call. They think I don't know what's going on, but I do; I see things when I'm up on those moors and it's more than just calling monthly for t'premiums and having a cup o' tea together.'

'Oh dear.' I didn't know what to say, so I added, 'Are you sure?'

'As sure as I can be when seeing things with my own eyes. Him waiting until he thinks I'm up on those moors miles away, then sneaking into the house, or her going to meet him at the gate when she thinks I'm working closer to home, or her going into the village for a coffee and being seen with him . . . It's going on all right, Matthew. It's not collecting the premiums, it's more than that; the times are all different. I know when he's due for the premiums, he comes regularly, but these are not that sort of visit. They wait till they think I'm out of the way. Now, like I said, I have no reason to think she's done owt wrong yet, nor would she, but folks can be tempted by smooth talkers – and yon chap is a smooth talker – so I'm going to bring it to an end. Stop him coming here before it all gets out of hand.'

'I can see the sense in that,' I said. 'But have you talked to your wife about it?'

'Nay, Matthew, there's no point in that. She'd only deny things and say it was all in my imagination. I shall just stop her seeing him, simple as that, without telling her what I've noticed. He lives far enough away not to come here without good reason, and we're a long way off the beaten track at our farm – it's not the sort of place anybody pops into when they're passing. I'll make sure she's kept too busy to go raking off to Baysthorpe or Guisborough or wherever. And I'll make sure the Land Rover's never available when she wants it. I'll soon kill their passion, Matthew, mark my words.'

I noticed he never spoke the NFU agent's name, but I knew it was Eric Newberry. His agency covered an area of the moors that was very similar to mine, and clearly a lot of the farmers had their insurance accounts with him. After all, his was a specialist insurance company for farmers and landowners.

Eric was a decent man and I found it hard to believe he was making advances towards a client's wife, beautiful though Jane was. Although we might be considered rivals, we were friendly towards each other and would sometimes meet, usually accidentally, during our rounds. On more than one occasion, we had shared a liquid lunch and a sandwich in one of the local pubs, comparing notes and benefits while grumbling about some of our clients. But he had never mentioned the Websters, and neither had I seen him anywhere with Jane.

'As you wish, Joe. Shall I start the ball rolling now? I can ring Mr Wilkins straight away to see if we can set up a meeting.'

'Right, that's the sort of quick action I respect.'

With Joe sitting nearby, I rang Montgomery Wilkins at District Office and he was at his desk. I explained that I had a potential client who wished to transfer all his insurance cover from the NFU simply because he felt the Premier was the better company. When I explained the extent of the cover required, Mr Wilkins was delighted and said he would like to meet Mr Webster on his farm as soon as possible, and he would bring an assessor with him. We agreed to meet at 11 a.m. the following Tuesday at High View Farm, Baysthorpe, and Mr Wilkins said he would collect me. In spite of my pot leg, he thought I should be present because this new customer was within my agency and I had been partially responsible for the introduction of such a good new client.

Joe was delighted and said he would look forward to

meeting us all at the appointed time. Before he left, I asked him to prepare some kind of paperwork ready for our arrival. It would need to be a full description of his premises, livestock, vehicles and equipment. If he had something from which we could work, it would speed the arrangements and help us ensure everything was covered. He said he had a list used by the NFU that they had updated every two years – that sounded ideal.

When Evelyn returned from collecting, she told me about her day, which had apparently been fairly uneventful, and then I told her I'd had a visit from Joe Webster of Baysthorpe, adding that he wished to transfer his insurance cover to the Premier, quite a major coup for me if it succeeded. Honouring Joe's request not to reveal the true reason, I simply said Joe felt the Premier could provide better comprehensive cover at a lower cost. I told her what I had done to begin the negotiations, saying that Mr Wilkins, myself and an assessor would be visiting High View Farm the following week to begin the negotiations. Because Evelyn was doing part of my work I felt she ought to be aware of the background actions that were necessary in such a major transaction – after all, she might be asked to do a similar task at some point.

'It's funny you should mention Joe Webster,' she said when I'd finished. 'I saw Jane in Baysthorpe shop today. I wanted some groceries, and thought I'd get them on the way home. We had a natter after we'd done our shopping.'

'You know her?'

'We were at school together; we were both in the hockey team. But I can't understand why Joe wants to transfer all his business to you, Matthew. He and his father before him have always been with the NFU.'

'You knew that?'

'Yes, Jane told me. We got talking about insurance. I told her I was doing your collecting because of your broken leg so she said you never called at their farm because they were with the NFU.'

'Right, but I went to see those two bikes some time ago . . .'

'She remembered that. But, Matthew, isn't it a bit odd that Joe should call today about a transfer? Especially when Jane just happened to mention to me that she wished you could call and talk some sense into her husband. Is something going on, Matthew?'

'Talk some sense into him? What does she mean by that?' I countered.

'Well, he's got his farm and everything that goes with it covered by the NFU, just as his father had done. They've been with the NFU for years with no problems. But he has no life insurance, Matthew, nothing planned for his pension, no investments other than the farm, no provision for him being off work for a long time through sickness or injury . . . Jane's worried about that and she's been trying to get him to take out those kind of extra personal insurances, but he won't listen.'

I realized now that during our conversation he had never mentioned any form of life insurance or sickness cover, and I had not queried that omission. I had just assumed his life insurance and sickness cover would be part of the entire farm package.

'So how does Jane think I could persuade him when she can't?'

'I think she was talking metaphorically; I don't think she wants you to interfere. She's trying to research various types of life insurance and investments without him knowing.'

'Really?' was all I could think of saying.

'Yes, she's having to sneak out of the house when he's not around, or fix meetings in Baysthorpe, all so she can have secret meetings with Eric Newberry, their NFU agent. He's produced several different options, some that she can opt to take out in her own name and others that involved the children or that might be in joint names, or just in Joe's name. The trouble is she can't arrange an insurance policy on his life without his consent or knowledge – he's got to sign the proposal form, so she's a bit stuck if he refuses point-blank, which he's likely to do. What she's trying to do now is get all the facts and figures put together, for a range of different options, and then present them all to Joe when he's in a good mood. She hopes he'll choose one of them.'

'How long's this been going on?'

'Dunno, a few weeks I think. You can see now, Matthew, why I think it's odd that Joe wants to leave the NFU, especially when Eric's really working hard to find something that will appeal to him.'

'But he has no idea Eric is doing all that background work, has he?'

'Jane doesn't think so, although she did say he'd been acting a bit strange lately. It's not financial worries, she knows that. She helps with all the accounts and their dealings with the bank. She's not sure what's upsetting him.'

My dilemma now was whether to breach Joe's request for total confidentiality and tell Evelyn the true reason for his wish to transfer to the Premier. I was confident he was mistaken about Jane's motives for seeing Eric Newberry. I know there should be no secrets between man and wife either, and so I had to find a way of putting to Evelyn the idea of Jane and Eric conducting an affair.

'Seeing Jane and Eric together like that would make anyone think they were having an affair!' I put to her in what I hoped was an oblique manner.

'Well, it's funny you should say that. She did wonder if Joe thought she was up to something with Eric. She felt sure he had seen her sneaking off sometimes to meet Eric and some of the village folks were a bit snooty with her after she'd had tea and scones with him in Baysthorpe's café. It might explain his odd behaviour.'

I lapsed into silence as I pondered the dilemma now facing Joe Webster. Having totally misunderstood Jane's actions he had begun a sequence of events that would benefit me through the commission I'd earn if he transferred to the Premier, but my conscience told me I should not take undue advantage of him in this way. To avoid breaching his confidentiality, I thought the solution was to ring him and ask him to reconsider his wish to transfer. If he had told Jane, she would have responded in some way, and so, if he changed his mind, it was not too late to cancel our appointment with him.

'I'm going to ring Joe,' I said to Evelyn.

'And I'll go and collect Paul, then get tea ready.'

When I rang the Webster's farm, Jane answered.

'Hello, Jane, it's Matthew Taylor from Premier Assurance.'

'Oh, hi there. I was talking to Evelyn earlier today. Sorry about the leg but it's nice she can help you by collecting.'

We indulged in a little small talk about our respective families, and then I asked, 'Is Joe there?'

'I'll get him,' she said, and then I heard her shout, 'Joe, it's Matthew from the insurance.'

'Now then, Matthew,' said the deep voice eventually. 'Glad you rang. Is there summat you want?'

'I think you should reconsider transferring from the NFU,' I put to him without any superfluous chatter.

'Aye,' he said. 'Mebbe I should. I told Jane when I got home and she went berserk; she's not seeing that NFU chap, Matthew. I was wrong. Very wrong. She's been trying to get me to take out life insurance, getting facts and figures ready for me. He's been doing research into various options. I reckon I might have to do that, it sounds sensible – take out a life insurance I mean, or a pension scheme or summat. Mebbe I should stay with the NFU for the farm and things, and do the life insurance with you?'

'I wouldn't want to take the business away from the NFU, Colin, not after Eric has done all that work for you.'

'Aye, well, I was going to ring you and ask if I could cancel our plans, Matthew. Sorry about all that . . . Can you stop those chaps of yours coming to see me?'

'No problem,' I said. 'I'm just pleased it's all worked out.'

'Aye,' he said. 'Me too. Look, you've been very decent through all this . . .'

'It's all part of the job, Joe.'

'I'll tell you what though. Jane was upset about me

thinking she'd do summat like see another chap behind my back, so I said I'd get her a present. I'm getting her a small car, Matthew; I can afford it. It'll be smart enough for a lass to drive in town in her best dress, better than my old Land Rover. So how about you doing the insurance on that? It'll be registered in her name but we'd like to insure it through you, just as a way of saying thanks.'

'I'll put a proposal form in the post tonight,' I said.

Eight

'The ladies of the parish have cast clothing of all kinds. They are available at bargain prices in the parish hall after the Sunday morning service.'
From a parish magazine

The above announcement in a parish magazine reminded me of the Victorian prudery that surrounded images of nudity. It is claimed the Victorians even covered the legs of armchairs because they might produce erotic thoughts in the eyes of those who saw them, and there is no doubt that a flash of female ankle was equally regarded as something from which the male's lecherous gaze must be averted. Whether this attitude stemmed from Queen Victoria herself is open to debate because the people were in the habit of copying the Sovereign in matters such as fashion, behaviour and opinion. If Victoria thought chair legs could be erotic then so would everyone else. It was much the same with the Alexandra Limp. In the 1860s, when Queen Alexandra was Princess of Wales, she developed a very painful limp through rheumatism in her knee. The ladies of the social circle surrounding her all began to imitate her limp, and thus the Alexandra Limp became fashionable.

This Victorian prudery, which was surprisingly widespread and which endured for some years after Queen Victoria's death, may seem strange in our modern society, particularly when, centuries ago, our great artists featured nudes, both male and female, in their finest masterpieces.

Even the Vatican, headquarters of the Catholic Church, has nude figures, male and female, within its walls, both as paintings and sculptures. They have been there for hundreds of years. Works by artists such as Michelangelo, Raphael and Leonardo da Vinci are just a few examples, with the Sistine Chapel boasting a particularly splendid display on its ceiling. One of Raphael's most dramatic works is also on a ceiling, the Villa Farnesina in Rome; it features nude men, women and cherubs, but with no hint of indecency. The nudity in those pictures appears to be absolutely normal and natural with no suggestion of orgies or any sexual behaviour.

This crushing British mentality continued for some years after Victoria died but after two world wars our behaviour and social mores finally began to change. Live nudes were permitted on the British stage, for example, provided they did not move; suggestive photographs of scantily clad women began to appear in magazines and newspapers whilst artists could exercise more freedom with their so-called artistic licence. Even now in the mid-1950s, however, the laws governing indecency still depended upon a mixture of common law, bylaws and statutes passed in Victorian times. Even if people's attitudes were changing, the laws of the land were not, and the vexed question of precisely what was meant by 'indecency' still remained.

One would hardly think this kind of problem would confront me on my moorland insurance round, but one morning I received a phone call from Jacqueline Pollard in her capacity as secretary of the village hall committee.

'Can I pop in for a word, Matthew?'

'Yes, of course.'

'I don't like to bother you when you're supposed to be recovering from that accident, but if you could spare a few minutes, I'd be extremely grateful.'

'No problem,' I assured her. 'Eleven o'clock?'

'I'll be there.'

Our paths often crossed because Mrs Pollard was secretary of all sorts of organizations, clubs and societies, as well as being a member of several committees; she was a hard-working member of the community whose mission was not one of self-gratification. Quite sincerely, she wanted to help the community. She arrived a few minutes early, and knowing she preferred coffee rather than tea, my kettle was already boiling. I made the coffee from a bottle of essence whilst she chatted about village matters, then we adjourned to my office.

'So, how can I help you?' I asked.

'It concerns the village hall,' she told me. 'This is rather an unusual request, Matthew, but we – the village that is – have been left a valuable oil painting. The legacy is from a Mr Richard Stansfield who lived in Gloucester; he was a retired solicitor with a large practice in that part of the country. He died about three months ago and it seems he was born and reared in Micklesfield, only leaving when his parents moved to Gloucestershire.'

She paused a moment as if expecting me to acknowledge the name, but I didn't. 'Sorry,' I said. 'I've never heard of him, it must have been before my time.'

'Yes, he lived here some time ago. Anyway, according to Mr Stansfield's will, he spent many enjoyable hours in and around Micklesfield, playing in the woods and on the moors, and attending events in the hall. He learned to play snooker and billiards here, took part in plays and the pantomime, went to Christmas parties, enjoyed the village orchestra, that sort of thing. He had lots of friends among the other children and their parents too; it was a very happy time for him.'

'So a gift of the picture is his way of saying thank you?'

'Yes. In leaving it to Micklesfield he wants it to be prominently displayed in the village hall and has even nominated the site. He has indicated he wants it to be hung on the south wall, midway between the stage and the main entrance.'

'Is anything there now?' I frowned as I struggled to recollect what was occupying that space. My memory suggested a few old brown-coloured photographs of the string orchestra, the prize-winning snooker team of 1911, the folk dancers showing their paces at a competition in Whitby years ago and some long-dead village worthies in wing collars and with heavy moustaches. In fact, I think there was also a print of Queen Victoria in all her regal splendour.

'There's nothing that can't be moved to a new site, except perhaps Queen Victoria,' she said. 'Our legacy is a large painting. It's in oil on canvas and has a thick gilt frame, so it will need a lot of space. I'm sure we can move any of the nearby photos and whatever else is hanging there, without causing too much fuss. In fact, it might be an excuse to put some of the older stuff in the loft!'

'So the village hall is going to be home to a valuable painting?'

'Which is why I am here, talking to you. Quite clearly, it will need to be comprehensively insured.'

'But the hall is already fully covered,' I reminded her. 'The existing policy covers everything – public liability, damage from whatever source to the structure, curtilage and contents, theft, fire, the lot. Every village hall has that kind of all-in cover.'

'This is a very valuable work of art, Matthew, and the committee believes it will need its own comprehensive insurance. According to the solicitor dealing with Mr Stansfield's estate, it is worth somewhere between six thousand and ten thousand pounds on the open market. And that is a conservative estimate.'

'Crikey! It should be in a picture gallery or museum,' I said. 'Not hanging in our village hall!'

'I couldn't agree more, but we must respond to Mr Stansfield's will, we can't ignore that.'

'So why is it so valuable?'

'It's the work of a German artist called Lukas Cranach who was born in 1472. Some of his early work was executed when he went to Vienna but it is believed this work was done in Wittenberg where he spent most of his adult life. It is thought it was painted around 1540 or so. It's a large piece of art, Matthew, about four feet high by two feet six inches wide.'

'I don't know his work. So what's the subject?'

'That's another problem.' She hesitated before adding, 'It's a nude. A young woman. He calls the picture "Woodland Nymph", that's the translation from the German, but it shows a totally nude girl lying beside a small pond in a darkly wooded area. Quite charming, actually.'

'I can see that's going to cause a bit of a rumpus when some of our more stuffy residents learn about it.'

'Because it's German, you mean?'

'No, because it's a nude.'

'Exactly, so for both reasons we need to have it very comprehensively insured.'

'You think somebody might try and harm it? Or even steal it?'

'Art theft is always a problem, but damage to works of art has been known,' she said. 'Pictures that have angered fanatics have been slashed with knives, chopped with axes, had paint thrown over them, set on fire, male statues have been emasculated, women's bare breasts covered up . . .'

'But this is Micklesfield!' I said. 'We don't do that sort of thing here.'

'Matthew, at least one member of my committee has already said she doesn't want the picture in the village, let alone hanging in the village hall. I'm not saying it's because she's a Methodist, but she does go to chapel and she's the sort who grumbles if a man wears a shirt with the buttons open even in the middle of summer. Anyway, the committee has seen photos of the painting and that woman thought it was obscene. I am sure others in the village will have similar reservations about it hanging in the hall.'

'Obscene? How can a work of art be obscene?'

'It's all in the mind, Matthew, like Victorians getting all worked up over chair legs. Some of these objectors must have very dirty minds! They imagine things normal people would never dream of. But she's got very firm opinions and has said if we do hang it, she'll resign. However, we must honour Mr Stansfield's will. We're obliged to hang it because that's what he has stipulated and that is what we must do. As I said, it means we must take out the necessary additional insurance. Which is why I am here. Is it something you can arrange?'

'I'm sure I can, but I'd better have words with my bosses first.' I was exercising some caution as I did not want to commit myself to such a major and rather specialized policy without obtaining expert opinion. 'I'll get back to you but due to its value, and the risks attached to it, I would expect the premiums to be quite high. Can the village hall afford it?'

'We'll have to! But that will be another problem, paying for the insurance.'

'You could always arrange a special fund-raising event to pay the premiums,' I suggested. 'In honour of Mr Stansfield's generosity.'

'That's one option,' she agreed.

We chatted a little longer and Jacqueline showed me photographs of the Cranach nude which I thought very modest and charming, not at all erotic, obscene or lasciv-ious. When she left, I telephoned District Office and asked to speak to Montgomery Wilkins, my Ordinary Branch Sales Manager. He listened carefully as I explained the situation and then said, 'The short answer, Matthew, is that yes, we can insure the painting. But, as I am sure your client and her committee will understand, there will have to be conditions.'

'What sort of conditions?'

'Mainly security measures. With a painting of that value on show in a place open to the public, such as a village hall, along with the additional risks you have mentioned, I would think our assessors would want it in a very secure container of some kind and bolted to the wall. They might even suggest putting it behind bars with a glass window so it could be on view while being protected, but all that will cost extra, and the premiums would not be cheap. Then there is the question of maintaining the picture – you might have to consider things like temperature control, infestation by pests and so forth. It will be quite a responsibility, Matthew.'

'I think we ought to put all this in writing so I can pass it on to Mrs Pollard, then she can present our comments to her committee before any further action is taken.'

'Yes, indeed. Leave it with me for a few days, and I'll get to work on it. But it does sound a good opportunity for the Premier! Well done.'

Within the week, I received a large envelope of official papers which included a draft of the proposed insurance policy for Cranach's painting. There was a range of suggested premiums, each of which depended upon the strength and type of security measures. To hang the picture in the hall with no security other than the normal locked doors and windows would cost £550 per annum, an enormous sum, but if the Premier's recommended measures were implemented, then the cost would drop to a more manageable £125 per annum. One problem was that the suggested security measures would cost a lot of money to put in place, but that would be a one-off payment which, once met, would only leave modest maintenance work. What the Premier suggested was that a large cavity, sufficient to accommodate the painting, be created within the wall of the building. It should be lined with metal and its door should be a metal grill with a stout glass front, capable of being securely locked. This would protect the work of art from theft or damage while still allowing it to be viewed. The proposals were very detailed with illustrations of the suggested 'cupboard', no doubt taken from the files of similar protection schemes.

However, the measures took no account of the reaction from those who did not want the painting on public display, but according to Jacqueline Pollard, the village hall committee was determined to honour Mr Stansfield's wishes by hanging Cranach's work for the benefit of the community, despite the protesters.

I telephoned her to say the Premier's proposals had arrived and told her that if the committee went ahead with the cheapest option, there would be some initial costs in meeting the insurer's requirements. She told me the hall's treasurer had a small contingency fund to meet any sudden and unexpected expenditure, such as the repair of a leaking roof, a falling chimney stack or repairs to storm damage. She felt sure that fund would cater for the necessary security measures. Having listened to my brief résumé, she said she would come and collect the papers, then call a special meeting of the committee to discuss the matter, particularly the difficulty in meeting the cost of insurance year after year. The executors of Mr Stansfield's will were anxious to have the painting delivered as soon as possible – it was currently being held in safe custody by his bank. When she arrived, she had a copy of the relevant paragraphs of Mr Stansfield's will, which she allowed me to read, and it was quite clear the village hall committee had no alternative but to display the painting. However, Mr Stansfield did realize the painting could be a form of valuable security for the hall and, if the worst came to the worst, they might want to sell it to raise capital. Inevitably, any village hall required updating as time progressed and ours in Micklesfield was no exception.

Even now, the toilets and catering facilities had grown hopelessly out of date, and the backstage area and stage curtains needed upgrading. Mr Stansfield had added a clause, therefore, to say that, after the passage of ten years, the village hall committee would have the option of selling the painting if it became necessary to raise capital in order to maintain the hall for the continuing benefit of the public. In saying this, it was clear that he intended the hall and the village to benefit from his gesture. Then I spotted something else of interest.

'He doesn't say he wants the painting to be on permanent display,' I pointed out. 'All his will says is that he wants Cranach's painting to be on show in the hall.'

'But surely that means it must be always on display?'

'He doesn't stipulate that, does he? He just wants it on show. I think if he had wanted the picture on permanent display, he would have said so, quite specifically. As things are, he leaves the options open. I think it's a very generous and thoughtful legacy, and it's up to the committee to decide how to make the best use of it.'

'So what are you trying to tell me, Matthew?'

'During our previous chat, you said we might have to have a fund-raising function to raise cash to meet the premiums,' I reminded her. 'They could be a drain on the hall's rather modest finances.'

'Yes, that's true. So are you saying that if we show it only once or twice a year, then the premiums would be reduced even further?'

'I doubt it, not if the picture is always on the premises. Even when hidden behind a curtain or in a safe or something, it is always at risk. One way of reducing the risk is not to have it permanently in the hall – keep it in a bank vault and fetch it out only on very special occasions, covered by short-term insurance. That might be possible and it should reduce the premiums. I could have another word with Mr Wilkins if you wish.'

'Oh, I don't think we could do that, Matthew; it would not be in keeping with Mr Stansfield's wishes. I am sure the committee would agree that it must always be in the village hall – and I doubt if any future committee would want to sell such a valuable asset. It is my view that we must find the means of paying the premium, year after year, and provide the necessary safeguards for this exceptional work of art. As you well know, the costs of the insurance will rise as time goes by – although I think the value of the picture will also rise. It will be rather like having money in the bank!'

Then I had an idea.

'Suppose, if the committee decides to build a secure container within the wall, that they add doors to it, with stout locks. In other words, the picture is not on show all the time, but only on special occasions – or even just one very special occasion. That might appease those who don't like the idea of it being on the premises. They wouldn't have to look at it and be upset by it unless they attended that one very special occasion.'

'Such as? What have you in mind?'

'I was wondering if, say once a year, the committee organized a Cranach Night. A grand occasion, an annual ball perhaps, with a top dance band and a splendid supper, a dressy event so the ladies could arrive in all their finery and the gentlemen in their black ties and evening suits . . . and the hall would need to charge a high entrance fee. It would have to be an all-ticket event, and there would have to be a limit on the number of tickets too. And during that ball the Cranach painting could be on show – but at no other time in the year. If you get the admission charge right, it would pay for the premiums and make a profit, and it would also result in Cranach Night being something very special – attended only by those who don't object to it.'

She didn't say anything for a while and then smiled. 'I

like the idea, Matthew. Thank you. I shall put it to the committee. Cranach Night? Micklesfield's annual ball – a night to remember. A very exclusive evening, one that would be remembered. Yes, I think the committee will go for that.'

'And I can give it a mention in the magazine!' I smiled.

The committee later carried out the Premier's recommendations, with generous help from local tradesmen who completed the necessary stonework, ironwork, woodwork and glazing so that the famous painting was safely installed. The lady who had threatened to resign from the committee changed her mind, believing a very honourable compromise had been reached. It meant she need not look upon the disgusting picture!

The first Cranach Night was an overwhelming success, a sell-out, with people rushing to obtain tickets, and for my part in putting forward the idea, Evelyn and I were given complimentary passes.

But even with free admission, the event cost us both a lot of money, much more than my commission on that special insurance policy. Evelyn had to go out and buy her very first evening gown and accessories whilst I had to find a suitable evening suit. We weren't accustomed to wearing such fine clothes, but I have to admit that without any such splendid adornments, Cranach's 'Woodland Nymph' looked very beautiful.

It was around the time of the early negotiations of that rather special policy that the *Micklesfield Magazine* was nearing completion of its proof stage. I had assembled all the contents, producing what I thought a well-balanced and highly readable magazine, with lots of local news, items of interest, a diary of events, personal anecdotes and memories, and well-planned advertisements for local businesses. I made full use of the alliterative letter M for the contents but had a little more time before I need present it to the printer. That allowed me time to give it a final polish, to iron out any minor problems, spelling mistakes, errors of fact and so forth. I would put it to one side for a few days, so that I could look at the contents anew.

In doing this I noticed an advert in my local Gazette for a furniture store in Guisborough, which declared: *Massive Sale – Last Week*. I wondered why it was advertising a sale that happened last week, and then realized it should have read 'Final Week'. Another report said *The dead man_lives in Middlesbrough* and yet another parish magazine announced, *For those of you who have children and don't know it, we have a nursery downstairs.*

Those were the kind of simple mistakes I must avoid!

It was around that time that, during one of my regular trips to his surgery, Doctor Bailey said it was time to have the plaster cast removed from my leg. This meant a visit to hospital where my much-autographed plaster was attacked by something like a miniature circular saw and then prised open with ominous cracking sounds. The plaster tore at the hairs on my leg to reveal a very pale and shrunken limb beneath. My sorry-looking leg was examined carefully and X-rayed before I was pronounced fit and well.

'I won't sign you off yet,' Doctor Bailey told me. 'But you can walk on your leg – in fact you need to walk on it to regain the strength of the muscles and you will find yourself limping for a while until both legs are equally strong. Don't drive your car for another couple of weeks or so – do as much walking as you can, with care, to strengthen the leg, then come back to me for a final assessment. Don't overdo it and let me know if there are any problems.'

And so with my plaster removed and my leg feeling as light as a feather, once I had dealt with my morning post and made any necessary telephone calls, I embarked on a daily perambulation around Micklesfield, usually just before dinner time. Even when attending my weekly session at the market, I kept moving so that my leg muscles would be exercised as much as possible. Meanwhile, Evelyn continued to do my routine, collecting in the villages of Delverdale, and as the time approached for me to resume my normal work, I knew she would miss her outings. In addition to the exhilaration of driving around the spectacular moors, she had thoroughly enjoyed meeting my clients, all of whom had made her most welcome. From my point of view, I would miss the luxury of spending more time at home, and watching Paul develop from a baby into a little boy, literally changing by the week.

To maintain interest and enthusiasm for my walking exercise, I started to explore those parts of the village I seldom visited. It was during one of those outings that I noticed a 'For Sale' sign at Alder Mill. It was on the gateway at the entrance to the track through Mill Wood. That track led down to the old mill. Alder Mill was totally hidden from the rest of the village; it was one of several along the banks of the River Delver. As the name suggests, it had formerly been a mill house but it had ceased to function as such long before the war. Alder Mill was deep inside Mill Wood on the western bank of the River Delver and it was served by a narrow mill-race that carried the fast-flowing water towards a giant wooden wheel.

That occupied a space on an outer wall and it had ceased to work many years ago, long before the war. Even in my childhood I had never seen it operating. Now, much of the wheel's timber was rotten but I had no idea of the state of the mill stones or the machinery inside the building. Having not been used for years, it might also be in a sad state of repair, although it would have been protected from the elements. Within my personal recollection, the house had always been unoccupied although it was furnished and there was a rumour in the village that it belonged to wealthy lawyer from London who came here occasionally for holidays and weekends. As a trespassing child, I had often peered through the windows yet I had never seen anyone in or around the house. I am sure it must have been used from time to time because smoke had been reported from its chimneys on occasions. Like lots of other children from the village, I played regularly in the woods, exploring the hidden area of dense and damp trees that grew even in the wetter areas of the river side – those trees were alders, hence the mill's name. Adults would also walk in the wood, for it was extremely pleasant, particularly on the very hot days of summer.

It was nice, therefore, to return to my old haunt, even if

I was now an adult with a son of my own. That day I had pushed open the wooden white gate at the top of the wood where the 'For Sale' sign had been erected. I then noticed tyre marks on the surface of the track leading down through the wood.

That track, wide enough only for a small car or a horse and cart, had an earth surface which made it slippery and rutted in wet weather but it was evident that day that a motor vehicle had entered the wood. I knew it could go no further than Alder Mill – the track came to an end at the old house, although there was a narrow footpath that continued beyond. It climbed back through the wood to regain the village about a mile distant but at that point was not wide enough even to accommodate a horse and rider.

As I descended through the quiet woodland, the steep slope made my weakened leg ache and so I took things gently, not wishing to risk further injury on the rough surface. Apart from the birds singing in the trees and the occasional rustle of small animals darting for cover at the sound of my footsteps, I was alone. Certainly there was no sound of a car or of people talking, but, judging from the tyre-marks I could still follow in the soft earth, the car had made only a single journey and the tracks looked fresh. Maybe it was the owner making one of his rare visits? I began to wonder whether I was trespassing, but felt I could continue – after all, I had walked and played in this wood for as long as I could remember. Indeed, most of the residents in the village had used that track without any kind of complaint from the mill owners.

As I approached the house with determined but careful strides down the steep slope, I could see a small light-brown car parked outside the garden gate. It looked like a Standard 10.

I continued, my curiosity now aroused, but there was no-one with the car. It took a further three or four minutes for me to reach the car, my intention being to pass the old house and continue along the little-used footpath back into the village, thus making a nice round trip. Then I saw another 'For Sale' sign in the garden of the mill house. As I was passing, a man emerged from the back door. I think he must have seen me walking through the wood towards the house because he was not surprised by my presence, and indeed appeared to wish to speak to me. About fifty years of age with greying hair and spectacles, he was wearing a smart navy suit and carrying a clipboard.

'Hey you,' he said, flourishing the clipboard. 'Can I have a word?'

'Yes of course,' I said as I came to a halt near the little car.

'Can I ask what you are doing here?' His manner was rather curt and almost rude.

'I'm going for a walk,' I said, gesturing with my hands to give him a sense of direction. 'Down here from the village, and up that path beyond the mill that brings me back into the other end of Micklesfield.'

'Don't you know this is private property?'

'The house and garden are private, yes, but the track is a public footpath. It always has been.'

'I would dispute that, young man. From the research I have undertaken, I understand the wood is private, and so are the garden and house, as well as this track that runs through the wood to the old mill. The whole of this woodland, in other words.'

'It's been used by the villagers for as long as I can remember.' I stood my ground. 'Anyone can walk through here and children sometimes go swimming in that deep pool, just upstream from the mill. Adults too, on occasions.'

'Do they, by Jove! And what about the quarry just beyond the mill?'

'Well, yes, we lads would play in there; it's been disused since before the turn of the century but the track goes right past it. After all, sir, both the quarry and the mill were thriving commercial concerns, the public needed access, and so this track is the one that was used. It's been used ever since, there's no way it could be turned into a private drive!'

'You seem to know your local history.'

'I was born here and still live here. I know which paths

and lanes are used by the villagers, and I also know that if anyone tried to block up a path or declare it private, there'd be an almighty outcry.'

'This isn't what I was led to believe.'

'Can I ask why you are interested? Are you the owner?'

'No, but I'm thinking of buying this old mill and the wood, and everything that goes with it. It's for sale, as I'm sure you know. I have a particular and very private purpose in mind for the entire complex. I was told by the estate agent, who'd got the information from the current owner, that the entrance road was totally private. He said the track through the wood, and the wood itself, had always been owned by the mill.'

'I think he's been a bit casual with the truth. Sorry to disappoint you.'

'No, don't apologize. It's the sort of thing I must know about if I am to make a serious bid for the mill. I'm sorry if I was abrupt with you just now, but honestly I thought you were trespassing.'

'Well, if you are seriously thinking of buying this mill, you need to do some careful research. I know of an Ordnance Survey map dating back a hundred years, and this track, right through the wood past the mill, is shown on it as a public highway.'

'So where is that map now?'

'The parish council has it in its files; my grandfather gave it to them. You'd need to talk to a Mrs Jacqueline Pollard. The man in the shop will tell you where she lives.'

'My solicitor should do that, but thank you. I might just look her up whilst I am here. And might I ask your name? In case I need to contact you again?'

'Matthew Taylor,' I said. 'I'm the man from the Premier Assurance Association.'

'Ah, good, then if I go ahead with the purchase, I know who to approach for insurance. I'm Gerald Lloyd, by the way. From Birmingham.' And he extended his hand to me, which I shook.

'Well, don't let me detain you,' he said. 'I must get on too. I'm making a note of the layout of the house, detailed measurements, scope for expansion, that sort of thing. With permission and a key from the estate agents, I might add! It is very private here, isn't it?'

'It's the quietest house in Micklesfield!'

'I can believe it, which is why I am interested. The house and woodland is not overlooked by anyone, that old quarry too – everything is cut off from the rest of the world. Just what I'm looking for.'

'Except for that public path right through the land!' I smiled.

'Absolutely,' he said. 'And that might be critical. Well, nice to have met you and thanks for putting me straight about this track. I'll do more research into it before I commit myself; I wouldn't want to antagonize the villagers.'

He turned away with a smile and I continued my walk, passing the old quarry and eventually following the course of the path through a rising meadow into the far end of Micklesfield. Although it wasn't a particularly long walk, I found it tiring and my frail leg ached but I felt I had achieved something worthwhile.

There were other little-used tracks around Micklesfield and I made a point of exploring as many as possible. Now it was time to make myself dinner – with Paul at his Aunt Maureen's, poached egg on toast followed by tinned rice pudding seemed a good idea.

The following Tuesday, I continued my exercise by walking briskly up to the post office to pay in the week's collected monies, and it was while returning via a different route that I encountered Jacqueline Pollard.

'Matthew, nice to see you out and about without your pot leg! How's it going?'

We had a fine exchange about the improvement in my mobility and then she asked, 'Matthew, did you by any chance talk to a gentleman down at the old mill last week?'

'Yes, we had a chat. I was giving my leg some useful exercise in the wood around the old mill, and he said he was interested in buying the property.'

'Yes, he called on me and said he'd spoken to you. He wanted a look at that map your grandfather gave us to put with the parish records. Apparently, it shows most of the roads around the village a hundred years ago.'

'Mr Lloyd thought the road down to the mill was private. I said it wasn't because it has been used by the villagers for years, and besides, it used to be the access to both the mill and the old quarry.'

'It's not quite so simple, Matthew. Apparently when the present owner of the mill bought the property, he also bought the old quarry, the woodland and the nearby field. When he bought it all, he also bought the road; it *was* private property, Matthew.'

'Private? But how could it be private if the public used it?'

'Both the current owner and the previous ones allowed the villagers to pass along that old road. Although the road was never a public highway, never maintained by the council, it was used by the public over the years, but the owner kept it private by closing it once a year.'

'So the walk to the old mill is private property after all?'

'So it would seem, although the owner can give permission for people to use it. It is known as a permissive path or restricted use route.'

'So is that man going ahead with his purchase?'

'Yes, he says he intends to. He's going to apply to the rural district council for the old mill to be re-designated as a hotel. At the moment it's a private house; it's not been used as a mill since the turn of the century.'

'He told me he and his clients would want to be very private, and the old mill was ideal.'

'Yes!' she said in all innocence. 'He intends to turn the entire complex into a naturist retreat with accommodation, like a hotel.'

'Is that what he said?'

'Yes.'

'Are you sure he said naturist?'

'Yes, I thought it odd he didn't say naturalist, that's why I remember the word he used.'

'Jacqueline, have you any idea what he means?'

'Well, I think he wants to turn the woodland and the

riverside, along with the old quarry, into a nature reserve, and then invite people to stay so they can study nature in quiet surrounds. That wood around the old mill really is full of fascinating things to see.'

'It'll have even more fascinating things to see if he gets permission to go ahead,' I smiled. 'A naturist retreat is another name for a nudist camp.'

'Nudist camp? You're not serious, Matthew.'

'Well, it would be ideal down there, wouldn't it? It's not overlooked at all. If he can prevent local people walking through the wood, he will be totally private, and I know of no law that says he can't allow nudists on his premises. The laws about indecent exposure and so forth don't apply to places that are totally private.'

'But we can't have a nudist camp in Micklesfield! What would people think?'

'I think we'd become a busy tourist centre!' I joked. 'But if they are well off the beaten track and never show themselves in public, what harm are they doing?'

'Well, I'm not sure what to think about this, Matthew. I must have words with the parish council; they might make representation to the rural district council to try and get this thing stopped.'

'The question of who is allowed to use that track through the wood could be crucial,' I reminded her. 'If the public continue to use it, then plans for his nudist camp might not be approved – that's if they need council approval.'

'I must look into this,' she said firmly. 'Yes, indeed I must.'

She stalked away upon her new mission and I turned for home.

It was inevitable that news of the proposed nudist camp reached the villagers and this was followed by angry letters to the press and to the rural district council, along with a protest meeting in the village hall; generally, the villagers showed their disapproval of the scheme.

There were some supporters, however, and many others who were non-committal, but a protester stuck a notice on the entrance to Mill Wood exhorting 'No Nudism Here'.

There was no doubt that those who made the most noise and created the most antagonism were against the plan; those who saw nothing wrong with it did not join in. However, one outcome of those small demonstrations was that groups of people made a deliberate point of walking through the wood at all times of the day and evening.

I wondered whether they went on such strolls as a means of showing the nudists they would always use that route even if the plans went ahead, or whether some actually thought the nudists were already installed and went along hoping for a quick flash of bare flesh.

That outbreak of strong feelings, quite uncharacteristic in Micklesfield, soon faded away because nothing happened. Gerald Lloyd did not proceed with his plans and did not buy Alder Mill. No reason was given but a wise old man in Micklesfield said, 'No-one in their right mind would want to go about stark naked in that wood, not among all those briars and with all those midges and flies about. They'd get bitten in some right fancy places!'

And so the great controversy faded gently into history and Alder Mill remained unsold. I did not benefit from selling an insurance policy, although I must admit I wondered how I might have arranged comprehensive cover for a group of nudists.

Nine

'Eight new choir robes are currently needed due to the addition of several new members and the deterioration of some older ones.'

From a parish magazine

B eyond doubt, the bulk of my new business came from those who bought motor cars. Since the end of the Second World War, ownership of a car, previously restricted mainly to the wealthier classes, was now open to most wage-earners, however modest their income. One reason for the increase was the abolition of petrol rationing and another was the rapid spread of instalment selling, otherwise known as hire purchase. It was also known as delayed payments, or perhaps more widely as 'the never-never'. It was a simple system: anyone wishing to purchase an expensive item such as a car, large piece of furniture, typewriter, gramophone, radio or even luxury item such as jewellery or an expensive watch, could spread their payments over a given period, say one, two or three years. In most cases, a deposit would be expected – perhaps ten per cent of the price – and the balance would be paid in monthly instalments, usually with a small amount of interest. In many ways it was a type of loan, but it did not come from a bank or money-lender; the system was operated by the shop, garage or company that sold the goods in question. The system was by no means new. It had long been used by building societies to enable people to buy houses – and indeed, it could be argued that the insurance industry had been using a similar system since before the turn of the twentieth century.

Payments for large policies had long been done by instalments. Even holiday schemes could be arranged by using the instalment system, just as funeral clubs operated in a similar way. Funeral clubs, with members saving up to pay for their own coffin, interment and farewell tea, involved payment of a small sum into the fund each month. For many years that had been a means of making sure one did not suffer a pauper's burial.

In the minds of some, however, the idea of buying something on the never-never was akin to borrowing money, and borrowing money was widely regarded as almost sinful. It was not the sort of thing done by truly decent people. The phrase 'neither a borrower nor a lender be' was often quoted by grandparents and parents as a means of teaching children to be prudent. The basic message was that if you wanted something expensive, you saved up until you had enough money to pay for it outright, without borrowing from anyone. Saving up for expensive items was considered merit-worthy; borrowing money wasn't!

With the instalment system, however, purchasers did not actually borrow money – instead, over an agreed period, they paid the required price together with the necessary interest. They received the goods upon payment of the initial deposit and made full use of them before the final instalment was paid. Detractors maintained that goods acquired in this way were not truly paid for – and therefore did not belong to you – until the final instalment. In their minds, this made it the equivalent of borrowing and therefore not acceptable.

In spite of older people's reservations, the post-war youngsters were not afraid of borrowing over a long period if it meant they could enjoy the finer things of life, and so the ownership of motor cars flourished, as did the acquisition of radios, gramophones and a range of other desirables, including expensive clothes and television sets. Married couples also made good use of the system to buy modern furnishings and contemporary furniture for their homes – gone were the days when they made use of hand-me-downs from past generations. Paying on the never-never had become very acceptable – but not by everyone!

One of the residents of Micklesfield belonged to the older generation who believed in saving up the full cost of any major purchase. He was Howard Redshaw, a stout florid-faced man in his early fifties who lived in a fine four-bedroomed detached house not far from the railway station. With a large garden and garage, it was his own property, but it had been left to him by his parents. That meant he had never concerned himself with the doubtful ethics of having to obtain a mortgage. Howard was known for never borrowing and never lending anything. His rigid attitude was not restricted to money but extended to the domestic routine so that his wife, Enid, could never borrow a cup of sugar from her neighbours or lend them an egg; neither would he lend his axe, hammer or lawnmower to those in need of temporary help. Howard believed fully in the adage of never borrowing and never lending, and he ran his household on that basis.

It was not surprising, therefore, that he did not own a car. He had never saved up sufficient money to buy one although, as a young man, he had tried. The snag was that by the time he managed to accumulate the necessary £50 or so, the price of a decent car had shot up to £65, and so his savings were never able to keep pace with rising prices. He therefore went to work in Whitby on the train where he was manager of a thriving furniture store. He did not own it but ran it very efficiently. The odd thing was that most of his customers now made their purchases on the never-never, yet it had not occurred to Howard that his livelihood and the shop's profits were a direct result of people paying by instalments. That was the modern way of spending and it had led to impressive success in commercial enterprises around the world. Meanwhile, at home, Howard continued with his rigid lifestyle without borrowing anything from anyone and never lending anything either. It must be said that he and Enid were very content, probably through not having debts such as bank loans, overdrafts and hire purchase payments to finance.

However, the couple had a son called Alan, an only child who had been bright enough to win a scholarship to a major public school, and then to gain a place studying law at Leeds University. Alan decided to concentrate on maritime law and upon leaving university had worked overseas for a while before obtaining a post with a specialist maritime legal firm in Scarborough.

For the first six months after obtaining the post, he decided to live at home and commute each day, a journey of about an hour, chiefly because good quality rented accommodation in the town was very expensive – even more so during the summer holiday season. The cheaper properties in Scarborough were used by holidaymakers and he found them far from satisfactory so, with his parents' consent, he decided to live at home for a few months. During the first months of winter, therefore, he had ample time to search for a desirable place of his own before the next holiday season began. This would enable him to search carefully for a property instead of rushing headlong into renting somewhere unsuitable.

I was not unduly surprised when Alan arrived at my house one Friday morning to ask if I would insure his car. I said I would be delighted and went outside to admire it – clearly, he was proud of his purchase. Although he had passed his driving test on a driving school vehicle, this was his very first car. It was a beautiful MG Midget in green with a tan-coloured soft top, spoked wheels and an external petrol tank on the rear, along with the spare wheel. Although second-hand, it was in remarkably good condition, with new tyres, a new exhaust and, so he told me, new brake pads, points and plugs.

'It's only done six thousand miles,' he said with evident pride. 'One careful owner in the three years since new . . .'

He was a tall young man, full of character and charm, and I could imagine him being a success at whatever he chose to do. Already, his life appeared to be happy and fulfilling.

Clearly, he had spent time seeking and selecting a suitable car for his daily drive to Scarborough, but at the same time it was evident he fancied a sporty model – it would be a hit with the girls, I was sure. When summer came, he could put down the top and show the girls its paces; an open-topped drive along the Yorkshire coastline would certainly be exhilarating.

In my office, I presented him with a proposal form and together we completed the necessary details. Everything was straight-forward, although he paused for just a fraction at the question 'Will the vehicle be kept in a garage? If so please provide the address.'

'Is that a problem?'

'Does it matter whether it's in a garage or not?' he asked.

'Security of the vehicle is one factor,' I explained. 'Those in garages tend to be considered safer than those left outside, and then there is the weather – radiators freezing solid in hard frost and bursting, ice forming in crevices in the body-work and damaging it, brakes getting frozen on . . . that sort of thing.'

'So the premium will be lower, will it, if it's kept inside a garage?'

'Yes, it all helps.'

'But it will stand outside all day when I'm at work . . .'

'But not at night,' I said. 'Your father has a garage, hasn't he? Is there room in it, while you are living at home?'

'Oh yes, bags of room. He hasn't a car, as you know.'

'So you'll use it?'

'Yes,' he said after another slight pause. 'Yes, I hope so. And I'll be looking for a flat with a garage in Scarborough; I've no intention of leaving my car on the street.'

And so I helped him complete the proposal form, explaining that, because it was an open-top sports model, the premium would be higher than a similar car with a hard top, and he accepted that. Another factor in his favour was that he was more than twenty-four years old – he was now twenty-five. A person younger than twenty-four years of age would have to pay a whopping premium for a sports car, which is why some dads put the insurance in their own name. One problem with that dodge was that the youngster did not accrue any no-claims bonuses so long as the policy was in Dad's name. Alan did not want his policy in his father's name – this was his very own enterprise, all of it!

When the paperwork had been completed to my satisfaction, he signed the proposal form and I issued him with
a cover note that lasted for thirty days. The garage that had
sold him the MG had graciously covered him with its own
insurance for a matter of a few hours to allow Alan to drive
his car home. I told him he was now covered by the Premier,
and so the garage's cover could effectively cease.

'So where did you find this little gem?' I asked.

'At Whitby,' he said. 'A small garage tucked away in a
side street above the railway station; it's got lots of sports
cars and seems to specialize in MGs.'

'Well, it looks beautiful and the body work is in tip-top
condition. I think you've found a bargain.'

'The price was reasonable but the terms were good too
– ten per cent deposit and the balance over three years, with
a one-year warranty thrown in. I reckon it's a good deal.'

I wondered what Howard Redshaw had thought about
his son making use of the hire purchase system. After all,
Howard had never been able to save enough to buy a motor
car of his own and here was his son, splashing out on a
lovely little vehicle because he had enthusiastically
embraced the instalment system to pay for it. Whether or
not Howard had any objections, Alan did not mention the
matter and I felt it was not my place to ask. Clutching his
cover note, therefore, Alan roared away in his shiny new
car and I wished him every good fortune with it. I knew
he would be looking forward to the summer.

It would be several months later, with a threat of snow
storms, frost and gales, that I was walking past the Redshaw
household having been to see a client who was away at
work during the daytime hours. Flakes of snow were already
drifting down to earth and it was bitterly cold. I noticed
Alan's beautiful little car parked outside the family garage.

I wondered if he had forgotten to put it inside for the
night but another answer might be that he intended going
out somewhere in the car, in spite of the weather. Whatever
the reason, I did think the little vehicle looked very forlorn
in the dark and miserable conditions.

I did not think any more of that incident until Alan's

certificate of insurance and policy documents arrived in the post. I rang his home that evening and Enid answered. She told me Alan was still in Scarborough and wasn't expected home until eleven o'clock or so.

'It's Matthew Taylor, Enid,' I told her. 'I've got Alan's certificate of insurance and his policy documents. Perhaps he could come and pick them up sometime? He'll need his cheque book too!'

'I'll tell him,' she promised. 'Will Saturday morning be all right?'

'Yes, I'll expect him then.'

When Alan arrived, I sat him at my desk and went through the details with him, explaining some of the smaller print about who could and could not drive his car on his insurance, along with other conditions, but, with his legal training, he said he was quite capable of deciphering even the most complex of clauses.

Then he said, 'Sorry I was out the other night. I was sorting out my flat at Scarborough. I've found one and want to get moved in before winter sets in. I don't fancy driving across these moors in a snow storm and, as you know, we're often isolated here if the snow's very deep. I wouldn't want that to stop me getting into work, so I'm moving in tomorrow night.'

'You've found somewhere. Great! I'd better have your new address for my records.' He wrote it on a piece of paper which I attached to his file.

'Yes, a lovely quiet flat, quite spacious and not far from the seafront. Handy for work too – and it's got a garage!'

'That's good news! It'll be somewhere safe to keep your car.'

'You seem to think it's important, keeping it in a garage? We talked about it earlier.'

'It's important if your proposal form says you are going to keep your car in a garage, that you do,' I pointed out. 'If something happens to your car when it's not garaged at a time it should be, then it could invalidate that part of your insurance cover.'

'Like what?'

'Well, suppose the insurance cover included a burst radiator. If you left your car outside all night in a hard frost when it should have been in the garage, and the radiator burst due to it being frozen solid, then the insurer might not pay out for that damage.'

'But I'd still be covered for driving on the road?'

'Yes, it's a case of reading the small print, Alan! I was reminded of that when I saw your car outside your dad's garage a few days ago.'

'He won't let me use the garage,' he told me solemnly. 'Mind, I have been using another one in the village most of the time, but yes, I did leave the car out one night. It was just that one night, I might add!'

'Why won't your dad let you use his garage if it's standing empty?'

'Because the car's not paid for,' he said. 'He's got this funny idea that everything that comes into his house must be fully paid for before it crosses the threshold, and that includes things going into the garage.'

'Did you tell him that leaving it outside could affect your insurance?'

'He said that made no difference; that it was my problem, not his. Besides, I did have that alternative garage, so it didn't really matter, the car was under cover. But he has his standards and won't budge. He considers it wrong to possess things without them being paid for in full, and he won't entertain borrowing to obtain them.'

'And yet he sells furniture on the never-never?'

'He claims he doesn't; he says it's the shop owner who is selling it, and that Dad is merely a pawn in the overall scheme. Even though he disagrees, he will do his duty for the sake of the shop, as he sees it. I've tried shifting his views, Matthew, but it's like banging my head against the proverbial brick wall.'

'Well, in some ways we must admire folks who stick to their principles in spite of everything, but in a modern world some principles can look silly. But don't tell him I said that!'

'I won't, but when I'm settled into my new flat, I'm going to invite Mum and Dad over for Christmas.'

'And cook dinner for them?'

'With a bit of help from Mum, yes!'

'I hope your parents enjoy the break.'

'I'm not sure whether Dad will. He'll have to sit on my never-never sofa, sleep in my spare never-never bed, put his feet on my never-never carpet, listen to his favourite records on my never-never gramophone and watch the Queen's speech on my never-never television.'

'Would he come, if he knew all that?'

'I don't know – except he'll never know because I won't tell him; I wouldn't want to spoil his Christmas.'

'I suppose that being in never-never land is better than being in cloud-cuckoo land,' I said as he left.

Because an increasing number of young people were buying cars on the instalment system, I began to notice a gradual change in the general appearance of Micklesfield. It happened because cars were parking in the streets, particularly at night. There was nowhere else they could be left.

Several village streets comprised long rows of terraced houses, each house having a small backyard with an outdoor toilet, and then a gate leading into a narrow back lane. That back lane was not wide enough to permit even a motor cycle to travel along it when a car was parked there, and none of the houses had a garage – they'd been built long before cars were invented.

With a kitchen and a living room downstairs, and a couple of bedrooms upstairs (generally without a bathroom), these were very modest houses, often rented to people who worked on farms and in local businesses. The parents would occupy one bedroom and the children, however many there were in the family, would share the other, with some sleeping on the landing or even downstairs in some cases. The bath was a coffin-shaped container of tin, which, when not in use, hung on a nail either in the outside toilet or on an external wall. It was carried into the house on a Friday evening – bath night – placed before the living-room fire and filled with hot water from the fireside boiler. All the family members then took their turn, the luckiest being the first because he or she had the cleanest and hottest water. The rest of the family had to wait in another room while the bathing took place.

With cars being parked outside the houses, it meant the rather narrow streets were sometimes obstructed, particularly if a large vehicle came along. Some horse-drawn vehicles were very wide, especially those used at hay time and during the harvest, and so a problem was slowly beginning to manifest itself in Micklesfield. We were beginning to suffer from traffic jams and this generated short tempers, angry exchanges and frustrated road users.

In some rural areas, road widening schemes were already under way, but this was impossible in the villages where cottages lined both sides of the street.

Quite simply the roads could not be widened and so other means of preventing traffic blockages had to be devised. Much of that responsibility rested upon the local policeman, who would threaten car owners with summonses for causing an unnecessary obstruction, dangerous parking or any other offence he discovered on or by the offending vehicle. A favourite tactic by the police, in both town and country, was to examine streets in which cars habitually parked at night because there were two important rules governing parking on the road during the hours of darkness.

The first was that all motor vehicles must be parked on the left or nearside of the road, and the second was that parked vehicles must always display obligatory lights during the hours of darkness. In general terms, this meant two red lights to the rear, two white lights to the front and two red reflectors to the rear. There were some exceptions for particular types of vehicle, but for motor cars that was the general rule. A further rule was that the obligatory lights must always being kept in good working order – the regulations said that 'every lamp must be kept properly trimmed, lighted and in a clean and efficient condition'. That quaint wording, a relic from the pre-motor-vehicle era, persisted well into the twentieth century.

In practice, local police officers would often be very tolerant about night-time parking, particularly in side streets and roads away from the main thoroughfares. They would not prosecute such motorists for parking without lights unless there was a good reason.

One good reason for issuing a summons was a complaint from another resident or perhaps a motorist, cyclist or pedestrian who had collided with an unlit vehicle. For a week or two after an incident of that kind, the police would show they were doing something about the problem by prosecuting all offenders on that stretch of road. The result was that all parked vehicles would, for a time, bear the necessary lights even if it meant their batteries running down so they would not start the following morning. Parking lights and weak batteries were poor partners, although push starting, or using the starting handle on a stubborn car on a cold morning, was a convenient means of getting warm!

In Micklesfield the problem had reached the ears of the parish council who in turn asked PC Clifford to resolve the problem by ordering the offenders not to obstruct the streets and to ensure they displayed parking lights during the hours of darkness. PC Clifford, who had to live among the villagers with his family, did not wish to be overbearing in his attitude to motorists. He had no wish to antagonize them into snubbing him and his family and so he would first advise the offenders upon how to behave, and then, if they ignored him, he would prosecute. He was as fair any constable could be.

In spite of everything, the parking problems continued and more tempers became frayed. In one part of the village – High Terrace to be precise – the matter was threatening to become very serious simply because the road was far too narrow for comfort if vehicles were parked in front of the houses. Then one Wednesday, when I was attending my weekly surgery with Evelyn, she advised me to go and sit down in the bar of the Unicorn because my weak leg was aching. She would look after my brochures and papers at the Jug and Bottle hole in the wall whilst I rested. The bar was crowded as usual, with few seats available, but I bought myself a pork pie and a pint of bitter, then noticed an unoccupied seat at a table. It was being used by Danny Randall, the garage owner, and Dennis Baker, our local builder. They were clearly having an earnest conversation but, in the middle of a crowded bar, it was hardly likely to be confidential.

'Mind if I join you?' I asked.

'No, help yourself, Matthew, sit down. In fact, you might be just the chap to advise us.'

'On what?' I eased myself on to the chair and settled down to enjoy a late snack.

'This parking business in Micklesfield; it seems to getting worse in High Terrace,' said Danny.

'So how does that affect me?' I asked. 'What advice can I give about that?'

'Isn't there something in your insurance policies that says cars have to be garaged when they're not being used? I know all ours are – mine, my wife's and my son's,' said Dennis.

'It's not a *condition* of a car insurance policy,' I explained. 'But if cars are kept in garages at their home address, then the premiums can be slightly reduced. Certainly the Premier likes cars to be garaged where possible.'

'I thought convictions also added to the cost of a driver's insurance,' put in Danny Randall. 'So if PC Clifford gets among those who park stupidly, and organizes a few summonses, it could put their premiums up! You can't beat the threat of having to pay extra as a way of making people adopt a bit of common sense.'

'Parking infringements and minor traffic offences like failing to light up at night wouldn't affect a premium,' I told them. 'It would have to be something like a conviction for dangerous or reckless driving, drunken driving, even driving without insurance, something fairly serious. If a driver notched up several convictions of that kind, then his insurance costs would be higher – if he was a very bad driver with lots of claims and offences against his name, he might even find himself unable to get insurance cover at all.'

'So we can't call on you, or the other insurance agents in Delverdale, to start putting pressure on drivers to garage their cars?'

'Sorry, no, we can't force them. But, as I said, if they do keep them in secure garages, then their premiums could be reduced. That's an incentive of sorts, if garages were available. But not all our local households have a garage.'

'Then let's build garages for them!' said Dennis. 'Now there's an idea . . . I could build two rows of garages, back to back, to accommodate . . . how many?'

'Depends on the space you've got,' said Danny. 'And I happen to own that field behind High Terrace. It's just over five acres and fairly flat, big enough to take a large garage block and a parking area with bags of space to spare. So how about us going into partnership? I rent you space in my field, and you build garages to rent to those poor devils who've nowhere to park.'

'Or I buy the field off you?' smiled Dennis. 'And get planning permission as a building site.'

'No way; I believe in hanging on to land. I rent it to you, so I get an income. You build the garages and rent them to car owners, so you get an income. That'll make both of us happy.'

'And I insure the new garage block so I get an income,' I said, joining this rush of enthusiasm. It did seem to point towards a solution and although any reduced premiums would not pay the rent, they would go some way towards the costs.

Dennis bought us all another pint as we celebrated our great idea. And it did happen – it took several months to get the necessary planning permission and plans drawn, but within a year, there was a smart new garage block behind High Terrace.

It was large enough to accommodate three dozen cars under cover, and a further dozen in the open air, but they were off the road and therefore not causing problems. Eventually, when the building work was complete, I was given the task of insuring the complex against all risks and PC Clifford helped to persuade drivers to rent the garages by regularly booking them. He issued summonses for not having the necessary night-time lights, parking on the wrong side of the road during the hours of darkness or for obstructing the highway. I was delighted he considered the matter so important for the overall welfare of the village, but felt his powers of persuasion were greater than my suggestion of reduced premiums.

I was always sorry when any of my clients died, but the death of Sebastian Clarence Braithwaite had been especially sad. It was because he was such a character, a real treasure and completely different from the local men. He was a man apart. He had been a loyal client of the Premier over many years, insuring his land, house, contents and car with us, and even persuading his friends and acquaintances to make use of the Premier as well. One of his regular features was to throw massive house parties in his huge home, all liberally aided by wonderful food and gallons of champagne, whisky, gin, wine and beer. The superb buffets were provided by outside caterers, with his charming wife, Lucy, acting as a most gracious and efficient lady of the house. In summer he would host these events in the garden, while in winter, they made good use of his spacious dining room and orangery.

Sebastian and Lucy lived on a small estate on the edge of the village. It comprised fields and woodland, in all about fifty acres, with some of the fields being rented to local livestock owners. The spread was interlaced with unsurfaced roads and a stream trickled through one corner. It was the next best thing to paradise and the couple liked other people to share their enjoyment of this beautiful piece of countryside.

Sebastian's *pièce de resistance* was to personally collect those guests who could not drive, and then deliver them home at the conclusion of his party, even after (perhaps) having rather too many glasses of strong liquor. In spite of his heavy alcohol consumption, he never had a traffic accident and somehow avoided being checked by the police. Most of his guests came from the Delverdale district and it was his practice to have at least two new visitors at each party; he liked to meet people not of his class and background. He was more than happy to introduce ordinary working people to the joys of expensive living, while not expecting or wanting anything in return. Evelyn and I had been guests on two occasions. I think his background was linked to the aristocracy and certainly he had plenty of money, which he enjoyed sharing with others less fortunate. His entire philosophy appeared to be geared towards having a good time and helping others to do likewise. And he did so in style.

One of the factors that made him so distinctive was his car. It was a 1923 Rolls-Royce, a 20 horse-power model with Mulliner Tourer coachwork.

It had an open top and the interior was large enough to accommodate five adults – three in the rear and two in the front. The paintwork was glossy black and its wheels were solid, lacking spokes or gaps, with the spare attached to the offside rear part of the bonnet. And, of course, it had the familiar Rolls-Royce radiator grille with massive headlamps and a flying lady mascot which some said had been added later. In this splendid machine Sebastian would sail around the village and nearby dale, waving to everyone and enjoying the fresh air if the top was open. The engine of this supercar was so silent that one could not hear its approach, and many a villager or visitor has been startled by the sound of its horn when it has crept up behind them. I was proud to insure such a wonderful vehicle.

More amazing than the car, however, was the fact that Sebastian was 92 years old when he died, and he was still driving the huge beast around the dale, and still organizing his fantastic parties. When he died, I visited Lucy to deal with those aspects for which I was responsible, such as transferring the necessary policies to her name and making sure Sebastian's life insurance was paid into his estate, for Lucy's benefit. In spite of her age – she was 87 – she was very alert and capable, and said she would remain at the big house where friends and staff would continue to help her look after the place and keep the garden tended. And, she insisted, she would continue with those tremendous parties.

One of the policies transferred into her name was that relating to the Rolls-Royce.

It had been issued with Sebastian's name as the policy holder and named the policy holder as sole driver. Lucy asked that it be transferred into her name, as the new owner of the car, until she decided what to do with the splendid vehicle. In this way she became the policy holder, and the clause that said the policy holder was the sole driver remained. I did not query this.

It would be about eight months after Sebastian's death that Lucy decided to host one of those famous parties, the first since his death. It was to be held on a Sunday in July, hopefully in the garden, and would comprise a buffet lunch with lots to drink. Guests were asked to arrive at 11.30 a.m. for noon. There would be 60 guests from various parts of the dale, including some from Micklesfield. Most, if not all, of those invited, had helped Lucy deal with the formalities and emotions of losing her beloved husband.

On the Saturday afternoon before the party, I decided that my Austin 10, little Betsy, needed her petrol tank filling, plus a pint of oil, and Evelyn decided to drive her to Danny Randall's garage. I went along for the ride, however, and so did baby Paul because we decided we would pop out for a drive and perhaps find a nice café where we could have afternoon tea.

When we arrived at Danny's garage, however, I was surprised to see Sebastian's Rolls-Royce parked on the forecourt.

My immediate instinct was that Lucy had found herself a chauffeur, and that he might be topping up its huge tank so that he could continue Sebastian's custom of collecting party guests. But when I went inside the garage to find Danny, I was surprised to see Lucy standing there, signing a chit for the petrol.

'Mrs Braithwaite!' My astonishment must have been conveyed in my voice. 'What a surprise!'

'Oh, hello, Matthew, how nice to see you. I'm just topping up for tomorrow; I have some guests to collect here and there. Seb would have wanted me to continue his custom.'

'Oh, I see . . .' I did not know how to react. Had she

brought the car down from her house? Or was there a chauffeur doing something inside the garage? I could not see anyone.

'Well, I must be off,' she smiled. 'Lots to do.'

And she walked outside, climbed into the massive open-topped Rolls, started the engine, engaged first gear, let off the handbrake and slid away from the pump with the car hardly making a sound, waving a grand farewell as she turned and headed for home.

'Did you see that?' I asked Danny.

'Amazing,' he said. 'Drives as if she's been doing it for years. I had no idea she could drive!'

'Me neither,' I admitted. 'And I don't think she's insured. How can I tell her?'

'Insured? Surely you've transferred the policy from Sebastian to her?'

'Yes, but she needs a driving licence. She's only covered by the insurance policy if she holds a driving licence. I'm sure she doesn't have one, as I've never seen her driving any car, let alone that Rolls. She wasn't a named driver on Sebastian's policy; he was shown as the sole driver.'

'I must admit I've never seen her drive either, but she looked very skilled and confident just now,' he said.

'My thoughts too, so how on earth did she manage to get it down here in one piece, without colliding with anything? Getting those cars started is a challenge in itself, especially for a beginner! But this is serious, Danny. If she's collecting people tomorrow, she really does need to be properly insured.'

'So you're saying she's really a learner driver? At her age? Driving without a licence, driving without L plates, no insurance! Don't let PC Clifford get his hands on her, Matthew!' And he laughed at the absurdity of the situation. 'But seriously, somebody needs to put her right before she does any harm.'

'It's no laughing matter, Danny. If she does hit somebody or collides with another car or causes one of her passengers to get hurt tomorrow, it could have serious consequences.'

'Then you'd better follow her home and tell her,' he said.
'Right, how much petrol do you want?'

'Fill her up please.'

And so, reluctantly and with feelings of real trepidation,
we drove away from the garage. At my request, Evelyn
made her way to Lucy's house while I explained the reason
for this slight diversion.

'Are you going to tell her she mustn't drive?' asked
Evelyn.

'What else can I do?'

'She'll be devastated; she really does want to continue
Sebastian's custom.'

'I can't allow one of my best customers to get into trouble
with the law if I can prevent it. I owe it to her,' I said, grit-
ting my teeth.

'It will spoil her party,' Evelyn said. 'Clearly, she's put
a lot into the organization so far, and collecting guests in
the Rolls is part of the fun, just as it always has been.'

'She can always hire a chauffeur,' I said. 'Money's not
a problem, and she can always find someone willing to earn
a few bob.'

Evelyn lapsed into silence as Betsy climbed through the
village to Lucy's fine property on the edge of the moors.
It was surrounded by a high stone wall but the main gate
was open and we drove straight through. Evelyn drove up
to the front door, the Rolls now being parked outside. We
halted and I climbed out, took a deep breath and rang the
bell. After a minute or so, Lucy appeared.

'Ah, Matthew. This is a surprise.'

'Sorry to arrive unannounced,' I began. 'It's just that when
I saw you driving the car, I thought I ought to remind you
about the matter of its insurance . . .'

'Ah, yes, but I am now the policy holder, as you know,
and according to the papers I have, that entitles me to drive.'

'But only if you hold a driving licence . . .'

'But I do, Matthew, my dear boy, I do. I've had one since
I was seventeen, but I have never taken a driving test. I
don't need to take one, you see, because I was granted my
licence before the first of April, 1934. And I have kept it

current. Do you want to see it? I have kept up my driving practice, you know, even though dear Seb would never let me take the Rolls out on the road. We've a lot of space here, good estate roads with lots of hills and corners, so whenever he was out I would take the car around the estate, just to keep my hand in, as they say. I did enjoy those trips, Matthew. And now I can take up where I left off, can't I? I must admit I am a little rusty with modern things like Belisha beacons, traffic lights and roundabouts, but I shall soon learn to cope.'

I did not know how to respond. 'I had no idea! Well, congratulations – I hope you enjoy your new freedom! I'm sorry to have bothered you like this . . .'

'Nonsense! You were just doing your job, Matthew, looking after me as I would expect from a good insurance man and a friend. I appreciate that. So I will see you tomorrow, with your lovely wife?'

'Yes, we're looking forward to it,' I said, wondering how the guests would react tomorrow when Lucy arrived to collect them.

Ten

'Remember in your prayers those who are sick of our church and our community.'
                                    From a parish magazine

With my leg getting stronger by the day, I was now increasingly mobile and this enabled me to complete my various tasks with much more ease and speed. One of those jobs was to finalize the copy for the *Micklesfield Magazine* and when I was satisfied everything was ready for the printer I telephoned Mr Cockerel. I confirmed that the magazine had expanded to twelve pages – his original quote had been for eight but I reminded him that I had telephoned earlier to check that he could cope with the extra four within the time range. He assured me it was no problem, although there would be a modest extra charge. I knew our increased flow of adverts would pay for that.

He asked me to pop the material in the post, suggesting I send it by registered mail to ensure it didn't get lost, and then it would arrive the following day, well within the deadline. In fact, I had made a carbon copy of all the typed work and so I could cope even if the original material got lost. Provided everything went well, the proof would be sent to me in about a week's time, and the magazine should be printed a few days afterwards. I was excited by this development – preparing the magazine for the printer had seemed a long chore with endless checking of facts, spelling, grammar and silly mistakes, but I had to admit I had enjoyed the experience.

I was confident I had not permitted any errors or laughable statements to escape my notice and found a sense of relief now that the project was nearing completion. It had helped me cope with my temporary disability and I wondered whether Ursula Henderson would resume editorship when she returned to the village. But all that was academic at this stage – Ursula was still caring for her sister in Lincoln and had not notified the vicar of any probable date for her return to Micklesfield. However, there was no immediate rush to prepare the next edition – if there was even to be one! If a monthly magazine was required, work should begin immediately, although I felt the vicar and his team would want to assess the impact of this edition first. Maybe a bi-monthly publication was the answer? Or perhaps a quarterly?

As Dr Bailey had not yet declared me fully fit to return to work, Evelyn continued to collect premiums throughout my Delverdale agency. There is no doubt my clients felt she had been a popular and efficient replacement and indeed her enthusiasm and honesty had generated a considerable amount of new business. This was especially noticeable through the increase of life insurance and endowment policies, the latter providing a means of both saving and making a profit from the interest that accrued over a long period. I wondered if perhaps we should continue with this arrangement. Officially or even unofficially! But that was a question for the future.

While she was away collecting in Lexingthorpe, I walked up to the post office in Micklesfield with the material for the magazine, along with several of my own letters.

There had been some notices of renewal in the mail from District Office and so I decided to post them to the people concerned. I included a covering letter saying the necessary premiums would be collected in due course and I also offered to help with any enquiries or problems that might arise, adding that I hoped to be back at work very soon. It was while passing Randall's Garage that Danny hailed me. He was topping up a car with petrol and oil, and spotted me walking past.

'Matthew, can you spare a minute?'

'Sure.'

'Go into the office and sit down, I'll be there in a tick.'

He joined me a couple of minutes later and offered me a cup of tea in a thick tin mug, greasy with handprints. I hadn't the heart to decline.

'So how can I help, Danny?'

'A bit of advice, Matthew. You know people now have more leisure time on their hands? A shorter working week and a bit more cash to spend, no worries about going away, no restrictions on travelling and no likelihood of suffering from air raids and bombs in towns and so on.'

'Right,' I said, aware that lots of working people could now take Saturday afternoons off work in addition to Sundays.

'Well, not all of 'em have gardens to occupy them, or some don't fancy spending their time decorating houses that don't belong to them. On top of that there's quite a few would like to see what life is like outside this village and beyond the moors that surround us.'

'You're absolutely right,' I said. 'I feel like that myself – I want to see more of England and explore further afield. And perhaps even overseas.'

'Then you know how folks feel if they haven't cars of their own. They tend to be stuck here. If they do go away, it means a lot of fuss working out railway timetables or catching buses one after another. I feel there is a great desire among ordinary folks to see more of the world, and more of our own country too. So I thought I would invest in a bus.'

'But we have a regular bus service,' I pointed out.

'No, I don't want to start a bus service; I want to organize tours in a comfortable bus, one with upholstered seats instead of wooden benches. Days out somewhere. Attract parties who want to organize trips for a bus full of friends, and groups of folks like the WI, church congregations, youth club or summat. I've given it a lot of thought – I could take bus loads to places like Blackpool, Bridlington, the Yorkshire Dales, the Wolds, the Moors, York – and I've always wanted to go to the Lake District. I've heard so much about it, all those lakes and mountains, but I've never been. Never had a chance. Mebbe I'll get there now, even if it is on my own bus! Anyway, I can give folks a really nice day out with meals somewhere, fish and chips mebbe or book a café for a sit-down dinner and tea breaks, then fetch 'em back home the same day. Or take 'em to a theatre or to see a show in Scarborough, a night out somewhere, a real treat. There's hundreds of folks living in these parts who will never get that kind of opportunity unless somebody does summat to persuade them.'

'Obviously you've given it a lot of thought.'

'Well, I can't claim it's an original idea, Matthew; other coach operators are already doing that kind of thing, but in this dale nobody has come up with the idea of doing short holidays or day trips by bus.'

'I'm sure there's an opening, Danny. I know folks do want to see more of the world around them.'

'I'm convinced they do. I'm thinking of day trips really, but I suppose I could extend it to longer periods – take a bus load to London and let 'em spend a couple of nights there, to see the sights and take in a theatre or summat. I can definitely see the potential, Matthew.'

'You couldn't drive the bus and run the garage as well!'

'No, I realize that. If I started by fixing the day trips for Sundays, though, I could do the driving because the garage is always shut on Sundays. And my wife could come along to check tickets and things, see to the arrangements for breaks and snacks and the like. Midweek, though, or for summat longer, I'd have to get a driver, mebbe part-time, or else get somebody to serve petrol and do simple repairs here if I wanted to do the job myself! There's plenty of chaps hereabouts who'd be glad of a few hours extra work once in a while. I think if I owned a bus that was going over to the Lake District or even to London, I'd want to drive it myself. It would be my chance to visit some of those places.'

'It all makes good sense to me,' was all I could think of saying. I could see he was very enthusiastic and felt sure his plans were sensible, not merely a sudden whim thought up without real consideration.

'Good. I wanted to see what you thought; you've been about a bit, in the army and so on, and on that motorbike of yours. Seen a bit of the world. There's plenty to see, is there? Up and down England?'

'More than enough to keep your bus busy. Or several buses busy!' I said. 'And Scotland isn't too far away, you know, or Wales.'

'I never was very good at geography, Matthew; I've never really known where other towns are. I mean, folks here just jump on a train when we want to go a long way, and it takes us without us knowing which way we're going. You just get on at one spot and get off at another without worrying which way you went to get there.'

'Well, if you're going to drive your bus to distant places, Danny, you'll have to get maps and learn how to use them. Any good book shop will have them in stock.'

'There's no book shops in these parts, Matthew! Not unless I go to Whitby or Guisborough, and I don't really have time to do that.'

'Have a word with Roger in our shop; I'm sure he'll be able to get some for you. He seems able to obtain most things. You need good up-to-date maps, or even an atlas if you intend covering the whole of England, Scotland and Wales – Ireland even. Your driver will have to know his way around as well, if you hire one, so he'll need to be able to read maps too.'

'Aye, I know that, but now the war's over and they've put name signs back on village and towns, and direction signs back on the roads, it makes things easier. I reckon I could find my way to Blackpool and back.'

'You'll still need a map, Danny! You'll be going to other places, far and near. You should never set off on a long trip without a map.'

'Aye, right, thanks. I'll remember that. Well, the other reason I wanted to talk to you was about insurance.'

'For your new bus?'

'Aye, well, it's not exactly new. It's second-hand because the firm who owns it has bought a brand-new 'un, so this 'un's up for sale. I've had a look at it; it's in real good fettle, comfortable and reliable, with plush seats and a set of brand-new tyres, new exhaust, regularly serviced and all that. Because it's a bus company that's selling it, I can buy it on the never-never, I can arrange trips that'll pay for it as I'm using it. Makes sense to me.'

'It seems a good idea.' I tried to encourage him, for I could sense a slight uncertainty in his words. 'If you buy it, you'll have to be sure to make it pay, won't you? Even if it means hiring extra staff.'

'Aye, I know it's a bit of a gamble, Matthew, but you never get anywhere in this world without taking a risk or two. So if I get it, can you deal with the insurance? Or do bus owners have to go to a special company? I heard somewhere there's a special system of insurance for buses, but I'd like you to have all my business if it's possible.'

'There is a special method of insuring buses but it relates to large fleets of them, or large fleets of any vehicle. It's called a certificate of security. It means that instead of taking out the normal motor vehicle insurance policy, the bus owner must undertake to make good any liability for third-party risks. If you do that, you are issued with a certificate of security – but in the case of buses, you have to agree to a figure of up to twenty-five thousand pounds.'

'Crumbs, there's no way I could agree to that.'

'No, it's for the big companies, Danny. One other way is to make a deposit of fifteen thousand pounds, which means you don't have to insure the vehicle in the normal way – but it means you have to deposit that sum of money! You're then issued with a certificate of deposit instead of a certificate of insurance.'

'No chance! I reckon I'll go for the usual thing, Matthew, summat straightforward. Can I add the bus on to my garage insurance? That already covers my own vehicles and those temporarily in my care.'

'I'll see what I can do, but you realize the premium will be quite high because your bus is a public-service vehicle? If it's used to carry private parties on special occasions, there are certain conditions to fulfil – they're in section twenty-five of the 1934 Road Traffic Act. Alternatively, you'll have to decide whether yours is an express carriage or a contract carriage, because the rules are different – there's quite a lot to understand, depending on exactly how your bus is used.'

'Right, it looks as though I need to do some homework first!'

'It's a good idea to have words with the Northern Traffic Area Headquarters; they're based in Newcastle and issue the necessary licences for public-service vehicles. They'll also tell you about the regulations affecting drivers and conductors. And you know a bus driver has to be at least twenty-one years old and needs a PSV licence?'

'Aye,' he said. 'I've got one. I need to be able to drive anything in this job, HGVs, motorbikes, buses, tanks, combine harvesters, invalid carriages – you name it and I can drive it. I'm qualified for all groups on my licence.'

'Good. But I suggest you write to the Northern Traffic Area of the Ministry of Transport, Danny; its address will be in the telephone directory and they'll tell you how to go ahead with the various licences you'll need for your bus. Then when you've bought it, come and see me and I'll fix up the insurance. I'll have words with my bosses in the meantime, just to be sure we're doing things correctly.'

'Aye, right, Matthew. Thanks.'

The outcome of all this was that Danny went ahead with his plans and eventually purchased a handsome 45-seater coach in purple and cream livery. It had been maintained in beautiful condition and was equipped with a heating system, upholstered seats with arm rests and even carpets. By the standards of the local market bus, this was indeed luxurious. Even before he had taken delivery or had an opportunity to advertise his tours and day trips, news of Danny's exciting enterprise had circulated in the dale. There is no doubt many people saw it as an opportunity to travel to places they'd never visited. One of the first to contact him was a lady called Cynthia Bristow who lived at Gaitingsby. She explained that her mother, Mrs Gloria Hodgson, was soon to celebrate her 75th birthday and when she'd heard of Danny's touring bus, she wondered if the whole family might have a day out at Lake Semerwater. Mrs Hodgson had heard about the lake and often talked about the legend that it contained a hidden village. Ever since she was a child, she'd wanted to see it. Her big birthday, with all her family brought together for the celebration, seemed a wonderful opportunity to see the lake, courtesy of Danny's bus.

Cynthia, anxious to please her mother and having pondered a suitable birthday treat, felt that a family outing on a bus was a wonderful idea. With 44 family members, a bus trip to Semerwater, with dinner and tea breaks on the way and perhaps a nice alcoholic drink or two on board the coach, seemed just right. And so she had come to see Danny. Having listened to her request, he thought it was a wonderful start to his new enterprise and became extremely enthusiastic about the plan.

I honoured my side of the deal by having all the necessary insurance details finalized in time for that outing, and Danny ensured that his coach had all the required licences and documentation. As Mrs Hodgson's birthday outing was to be on a Sunday and it was also his very first booking, Danny decided that he would drive, his wife would accompany him and he would provide a few bottles of champagne for the family, as a treat.

It would be a celebration for everyone. Danny's wife had made advance arrangement to halt at a pub at noon for a leisurely dinner and had ordered 46 meals with Yorkshire pudding followed by roast beef, carrots, peas and mashed potato and rice pudding to finish. It all sounded quite wonderful.

Because the outing was to be in September, the day would be long with ample daylight, so they could take advantage of the summer by having an early start. And so it was that, at 8 a.m. that Sunday morning, Danny's bus departed from his garage, shining in its highly polished livery, and it called at various houses in and around Micklesfield to collect the relations of Mrs Bristow's mother, along with the old lady herself. And then, shortly after eight-thirty, it started its journey, chugging sedately up Delverdale, leaving its narrow lanes to cross the Hambleton Hills towards the Vale of Mowbray and eventually Lake Semerwater.

Later that day, as Evelyn and I were taking Paul for a walk around the village, hoping to feed some of the ducks at the riverside, we encountered several villagers all taking their Sunday afternoon strolls. One or two asked after my leg, which was clearly almost healed because I was no longer limping, and then, on the riverbank, we met Jacqueline Pollard and her husband, Raymond, also enjoying a walk in the summer sunshine. We stopped for a chat as Paul threw pieces of bread into the water for the greedy ducks.

Then Mrs Pollard, who knew about most of the things that were happening in Micklesfield, said, 'I was so pleased for Mrs Bristow, when she managed to hire Danny's new bus for her mother's big day. He was so pleased she had booked the first outing and that he could drive them; he's always wanted to visit the Lake District.'

'Oh, he's not going there,' I said. 'Not on this trip, it's just to Lake Semerwater.'

'Isn't that in the Lake District?' she asked with surprise.

'No, it's in the Yorkshire Dales, high in Wensleydale and not far from Hawes. In the North Riding of Yorkshire, not the West Riding dales, but deep in the Pennines. Beautiful and serene in the hills. I went on my bike once, when I was younger. It's about an hour and a half's drive from here. I thought they'd head towards it, stop for a tea break somewhere en route and get to Semerwater before dinner-time. There's not much to see once you get there, so they could have a walk around, then have dinner at a local pub and head for home during the afternoon while seeing something of the Yorkshire Dales, perhaps with a break at Leyburn or Masham on the return journey. A really nice day out.'

'Oh my goodness!' She clasped a hand to her mouth. 'I'm sure Danny said he was going to the Lake District today, that's why he set off so early. It's over a hundred miles, he told me, so he wanted a good start. He was very excited about the whole thing.'

'I know he was delighted that his bus was being used for a birthday party, but I had no idea he thought Semerwater was in the Lake District.'

'It's the one place he's always wanted to go, and this seemed the perfect occasion for him – and he could take an old lady to see the lake she'd always wanted to visit.'

'Well,' I said, 'a lot depends on which way he's gone. If he goes up Wensleydale to the Lake District, he'll pass very close to Semerwater. If there are signposts for the lake, he'll find it, I'm sure, but if he goes over Bowes Moor along that old Roman road above Richmond, he'll never pass anywhere near it.'

'They were going to stop at a pub for dinner,' she added. 'Oh dear, I wonder if Danny really knows where he's going!'

I recalled our earlier conversation about his lack of knowledge of the geography of England and the fact that he didn't seem to have a map in the house, but it was too late now. But if the bus full of revellers did not appear at the pub for Sunday roast beef and Yorkshire pudding, the management would not be too pleased. Danny could finish up with a hefty bill for a dinner they never ate, not to mention more than forty hungry, angry people miles away from home. I felt a twinge of sympathy for Danny because it was so important that his first outing was a huge success – but this one had all the signs of being a disaster. But there was nothing anyone could do now.

News of Danny's disappearance into the great unknown flashed around the village that afternoon, with no-one really knowing where he'd actually gone. Within a very short time, stories of that kind tend to reach the ears of everyone within a small community and so those of us who were aware of the problem maintained a watching brief throughout the remaining part of the afternoon and into the evening. Neighbours living nearby maintained a careful watch so they could inform the rest of us because there was quite a lot of genuine concern for the absent passengers. There was even a suggestion – or perhaps just a rumour – that the bus had either been involved in an accident or suffered a major breakdown, although no such news actually reached us. Then finally we heard Danny and his passengers had returned, safe and sound. It was almost ten o'clock when his bus eased into his garage, having deposited its customers at their homes in and around Micklesfield. I could almost sense the collective sigh of relief.

I was one of those who wondered where Danny had got to on the day and so, anxious to determine whether there had been a major problem, I took the opportunity to ask him next time I called in for petrol.

'How was the trip to Semerwater?' I asked as casually as possible.

'Wonderful!' he said. 'Absolutely wonderful, Matthew, a real celebration, a right good start to my new enterprise.'

'You got to Semerwater then?'

'Oh aye, after a bit of tour round. Mebbe I should have had a map like you said, but when I said I was going to the Lake District with a bus trip, a pal of mine recommended a good pub for dinner. The Lion at Gatebeck. So Anita rang and booked us all in. The pub landlady told us how to find the place. It was near Windermere, so I thought that would be great – we could have summat to eat and then have a ride round the lakes – Windermere, Grasmere, Thirlmere, Ullswater, Derwentwater, the lot.'

'But Semerwater is nowhere near the Lake District!' I pointed out.

'I know that now, Matthew, but I didn't know it then. I must admit I thought it was one of those in the Lake District. So off we went with me looking for Semerwater among all those other lakes. There's no wonder I couldn't find it. I even bought a map of the Lake District and the north of England when I was over there because nobody could tell me how to find Semerwater. But, by gum, what lovely countryside! I've never seen so many lakes – eight or ten miles long some of 'em.'

'So the pub was in the Lake District? You had to go all that way for your dinners?'

'Aye, as I said, it's not far from Windermere. A lovely spot, mark you, and they did wonderful Yorkshire puddings.

It's not often you get decent Yorkshire puddings once you're out of Yorkshire, but that spot knew how to cook 'em.'

'So what about Mrs Hodgson and her wish to visit Semerwater? You know it's in Wensleydale, not far from Hawes?'

'Oh, aye, I found it eventually, on those maps I bought. It was only two or three miles off our return route, so we all stopped there on the way back. It was still daylight so we had a potter around and drank some more champagne to wish Mrs Hodgson many happy returns whilst we were all at Semerwater. Actually, most of the others were past caring by this time; they'd drunk all my champagne and brought a few bottles of their own, with some beer and Martini as well. There was quite a party on that bus. Then we stopped again at Middleham; there's a nice little café in the market place where we got summat else to eat and drink for supper. We all had a great time, Matthew. Especially Mrs Hodgson. She's never seen so many lakes and she even managed a paddle in Semerwater. She never found that sunken village though, but she wants to go back when the water's lower.'

'I'm pleased everything turned out well.' I was relieved at his news. 'So other folks will be wanting to hire your bus?'

'Oh aye, I've had a few enquiries already, but I am getting myself set up with maps, Matthew. You were right; it's a good idea to know where you're going before you set off!'

'I couldn't agree more,' I said, leaving him to bask in his glow of satisfaction.

A few minutes later, I went into the shop to pay my newspaper bill and the 75-year-old birthday girl, Gloria Hodgson, was also there, doing her weekly grocery shopping.

'Hello, Mrs Hodgson,' I greeted her. 'They tell me you had a great day out on Danny's bus last week.'

'Wonderful,' she beamed. 'Quite wonderful – all those lovely lakes and a paddle in Semerwater too! You know, Mr Taylor, until then I had no idea the world was such a big place.'

*   *   *

Meanwhile the printed proofs of the *Micklesfield Magazine* arrived through the post. There were two copies and, when checked, one copy was required back with the printer in no later than a week's time. I felt the vicar should check one copy so that there was an independent examination – sometimes one did not notice one's own mistakes, particularly after spending so much time on the job. As I was continuing to exercise my leg by walking as much as possible, I decided to walk up to the vicarage to leave a copy with him. I telephoned in advance to ensure he would be at home and so, that Thursday morning, I arrived at 11 a.m. The vicar, Jeremy Salter, invited me into his study for a coffee made from essence and I explained my requirements.

'I'll let the parish council have a look at it too,' he offered.

'Can I suggest you don't let them? The more people who look at it now, the more changes they'll want. I'd like you to look through to see if you can spot any printing errors or other mistakes. You'll see I've expanded it to twelve pages, all full, and the adverts will cater for the extra printing costs. I must return it to the printer as soon as possible.'

He smiled. 'I see you understand parish councils better than I thought. I'll read it today, Matthew, and you'll have it back this afternoon.'

'I was wondering whether we should put a cover price on it,' I suggested. 'There is a well-known theory, especially among Yorkshire folk around here, that summat for nowt is never a good idea. If you pay a fair price for it, that will be respected. And some people might not want the magazine thrust upon them!'

'The snag with charging a cover price, Matthew, is that someone must take the money and be responsible for it. It adds to the work load. I'd like to see what kind of reception this magazine gets, and that will decide whether we do another.'

'Fair enough, so we'll let this one go to anyone who wants it, free of charge. But can I suggest I don't print enough copies for everyone?'

'Not enough?'

'If they think there's not enough to go around, they'll all want one, and if we do another issue, they'll make sure they order theirs before they all disappear! We don't want copies hanging around the shops and pub unwanted. We have to create a demand, Jeremy. That won't work if there are too many spares.'

'I like the idea, so yes. And we mustn't print one for every person in the village anyway; we should be aiming for one per household.'

'Less ten per cent,' I laughed. 'To create a shortage!'

'All right, I'll go along with that. Not quite enough for everyone . . . I'll make sure everyone knows that. And you're sure the adverts will cover the cost of printing?'

'Yes, I've done my sums and there should be a small profit which could be put into a bank deposit account when we've got it all in. We'll need to send out invoices to the advertisers.'

'Can you do that?'

'I can, provided the doctor doesn't sign me off sick leave just yet. Another week off work would be fine.'

Together we scanned through the magazine's layout and Jeremy expressed his pleasure at its general appearance. I explained that all the advertisers had been sent copies of their adverts, just as a final check, and I hoped none would withdraw at this late stage. Often, especially when organizing a group of people for a dinner or conference, one or two dropped out at the very last minute, and someone always wanted to join in at the last minute. Those last-minute adjustments cause a lot of work for any organizer, but so far, all my advertisers had confirmed their wish to be included. I left the vicarage with Jeremy's promise to return the proofs to me later in the day.

It was while walking back home that I noticed Dr Bailey emerging one from of his patients' houses. He spotted me and beckoned.

'Ah, Matthew, just the chap. I was going to pop in to see you later today but I can deal with it here. I need to examine your leg – you seem to be walking very well now and I think I could possibly sign you off the sick list. How about seeing me tomorrow morning? Nine-thirty at the surgery?'

'Yes,' I said. 'No problem. I'll be there. And I'll walk.'

As we chatted, I confirmed that my leg appeared to be completely healed, adding that I was no longer suffering from pain and tiredness as I exercised it around Micklesfield. We had a chat about village matters – he'd heard about the forthcoming magazine – and then we parted and went our separate ways. It looked as if I would be back at work very soon!

As I approached my home, I noticed a black Morris Oxford parked outside and, as I reached the back door, a man emerged from the car.

'Ah,' he said. 'Are you Matthew Taylor, the insurance man?'

In his mid-forties, I estimated, he was tall and lithe with a head of blond hair, and was smartly dressed in a grey suit.

'Yes.'

'Richard Whitlock from Whitby,' he said by way of introduction. 'I used to live here as a child – in fact my parents are still here, Stan and Mary. In Oak Tree Cottage, at the top end of High Terrace.'

'Ah, yes, I know them.'

'Good customers of yours, so they tell me. Well, sorry to arrive unannounced but I was in the village, seeing my folks, and thought I'd pop in. I'd welcome a chat.'

'Come in,' I invited and led him through to my office. I offered him a cup of tea but he declined, saying he was heading to his parents for dinner. His mother insisted they sat down precisely at twelve, so he didn't want to be late. 'So how can I help you?'

'It's about insurance. I've bought a ship.'

'A ship?'

'Well, not an ocean liner or a disused warship or anything. It's an old paddle streamer in full working order; it'll seat about fifty people and is fully equipped with a galley, seating accommodation under cover with glass windows and a small bar. It's been used since Victorian times until just before the war. It was on the Thames to carry posh people up and down the river for parties and sight-seeing, visiting regattas and so on.'

'Nice for some!' I chipped in.

'They knew how to live in those days! Anyway, it fell into disuse during the war and has never been reinstated. I found it in a breaker's yard; I think the chap didn't want to see it broken up. It needs a bit of work to fully restore it but when all that's done, it will be a real gem. It contains some gorgeous woodwork and brass fittings, all in remarkable condition.'

'Obviously there was a reason for you buying it!'

'Yes, I intend to use it at Whitby. With people having more leisure time, I want to operate it from Whitby, taking passengers out to sea for short trips along the coast, or letting people hire the boat as a whole for parties, anniversaries, wedding receptions and so forth.'

I told him about Danny's bus project and he said his idea was very similar, except that it was sea-borne.

'So how can I help?'

'Insurance, Mr Taylor. My parents have always told me how professional you are, but I will be honest and say I have approached several Whitby insurance offices, but no-one will take me on; they all said I need to approach a specialist.'

'That's right, it's because the insurance of commercial ships and boats is a very specialized area,' I said. 'Maritime insurance is quite different from that associated with land-based properties, businesses, vehicles and people. It's governed by the Maritime Insurance Act and specialist brokers will handle the matter, before putting you in touch with a suitable company. They'll find the right insurer for you.'

'So you can't help either?'

'All I can do is offer to find the nearest maritime broker for you but if I approached my own company, they would simply do the same. Maritime specialists don't involve themselves with land-based insurances – they cover what are known as maritime perils.'

'Which are?'

'Things included in the Maritime Insurance Act. Perils of the seas, fire, war perils, pirates, rovers, thieves, captures, seizures, restraints and detainments by princes and peoples, jettison, barratry – and all other perils including collisions, bursting boilers and marine losses. And much more! Those are hardly the kind of thing a land-based insurance company could cope with!'

'Right, I understand now. You'd think those Whitby offices would have explained that to me.'

'If it was just a clerk sitting behind a desk, I doubt if he or she would know where to find the specialists. Most seafarers know that already and don't approach land-based insurers.'

'I understand; I must admit I didn't press them further or ask to see a senior person. Maybe I should have done?'

'There should be a specialist maritime agent in Whitby, or in one of the other nearby ports. I can check for you.'

'No, I'll do it. I need to stand on my own two feet! This is a new venture and I want to learn as much as I can about it. I've already learned something by coming here today. Now, there is one other thing. My parents tell me you are compiling a village magazine. I was wondering if you take adverts? I need to advertise my new enterprise in advance, as widely as possible.'

'There's no room in this issue,' I said, and I showed him the proofs to confirm my statement.

I felt as if I was not giving the poor man very good service today! 'I'm full up, every inch of space taken, but there might be another issue soon – can you wait?'

'I would have liked an early announcement in this issue, but I understand. I'm missing the boat, aren't I?' he joked. 'Is there likely to be a vacancy, at the last minute?'

'That's always a possibility but I know of none at the moment,' I admitted. 'Nothing is certain, but if there is, can I get in touch with you? If someone does drop out, there would be room for whatever space is made vacant, provided the printer hasn't gone to press. I'm talking of a matter of days here, not weeks.'

'Right, I'll settle for that,' he said, and scribbled his telephone number on a piece of paper which I popped into the file with the other magazine material. 'No matter how short the time, give me a ring if there's space for me.'

I was sorry I could not help him with the insurance of his craft but I felt he understood it was a very specialized type of cover, not to be conducted by land-lubbers like me.

Once he'd gone, I settled down to read the proofs of the *Micklesfield Magazine* and, although I spotted one or two minor printing errors, which would be easily rectified, the rest of the work was faultless. All I had to do now was await the vicar's response and then I could get a marked proof into the post – with publication set for next week. He was true to his word and arrived early that afternoon. When he delivered his copy, he had found the same errors I had, and nothing else. That was very good news. I managed to catch the evening post and settled down to await the final product.

In the meantime, however, the doctor wanted to examine me and my leg. It looked almost certain I would be back at work either next week or the one following. When I visited Dr Bailey, he made me do some exercises, asked a few questions, tested my reactions by tapping my knee and then signed me off the sick register with effect from a week on Monday. He also said I could drive my car again. It meant my life would return to normal after what had proved to be a fascinating few weeks.

It was on the Monday of my final week of sick leave that I received an urgent phone call from one of the advertisers in the *Micklesfield Magazine*.

'Mr Taylor, it's Erica from Baxter's Home Stores. You have an advert from me, for the Micklesfield Magazine. Am I too late to cancel it?'

'Cancel it? Oh dear, it's at the printers now, I've no idea how close to publication he is.'

'It's just that we've sold out to a large store in Scarborough; they've taken all our stock and offered me a post as manager, so Baxter's has closed. A week ago. I should have told you earlier but forgot in the middle of coping with everything else. I thought I'd ring now on the off-chance I could halt the advert; I don't want customers going to a shop that doesn't exist.'

'I'll see what I can do,' I promised.

'I'll pay for the space,' she offered. 'It's not fair on you that I'm pulling out, but I must think of my customers.'

I made a note of her telephone number and promised to call back when I'd spoken to Mr Cockerel at the printers. He was most accommodating and said there was time to cancel the advert, but it would leave a blank square on the bottom right corner of the inside back page. That did not bother him too much, he told me, because he could print a notice in the space, offering it to someone in the next issue while highlighting the value of local advertising. Even with one advert missing, the costs of printing would still be covered. I decided not to press Baxters for the fee. I felt that was a good compromise but added that I might have a customer who was interested – I was thinking of Richard Whitlock and his pleasure boat.

'This sort of thing happens all the time, Mr Taylor,' he said placidly. 'We've a day or two left – as they say, when an advertising space becomes vacant, someone usually wants to fill it!'

'Could you cope with a last minute advert?'

'I could even fit one in while the compositor is at work,' he said with a hint of humour in his voice. 'So if someone wants to fill that space, don't be frightened to call. The day after tomorrow is the final deadline for me, preferably before noon.'

I rang Richard Whitlock's number straight away but got no reply and after several unsuccessful attempts, I thought I would try again tomorrow.

Meanwhile, I wrestled with the idea of returning to work full-time, with Evelyn having to give up the routine she had truly enjoyed out and about in Delverdale.

Early the following morning I tried Richard Whitlock again. This time he answered.

'Ah, Mr Whitlock, it's Matthew Taylor from Mick-lesfield. I have a last-minute cancellation for an advert in that magazine we talked out. It's only a two-by-two-inch square on the inside of the back page, but it's become vacant. It's available if you want it.'

'Wonderful! Right, yes, I'll take it. What's the cost?'

'It's only ten shillings for one issue but we need to contact the printer this morning. We're talking about a couple of dozen words or so at the most. Fewer words means we can use bigger lettering. Maybe you could design your own advert?'

'Right, I'll get cracking straight away,' he said without hesitation.

'I'll ring him and tell him it's on the way,' I offered. 'Maybe he'll hold the presses until he's got the wording.'

'Look, why don't I ring him direct? That'll save time and he can tell me what space is left, if any, and we can discuss print sizes and so on.'

'Right,' I agreed, slightly worried that I would not be able to check the wording for errors. I really did want to produce an error-free magazine but due to the shortage of time, I provided Mr Cockerel's telephone number.

As I was now allowed to drive my car once more, I found myself driving across the moors to Guisborough to collect the printed copies. It had been a lengthy task but very rewarding, and I was dying to see the finished result. I collected my box of magazines and the first thing I did was to pick out one of them and turn to the back page. I wanted to check Mr Whitlock's advert – the only item I had not checked or proofread myself. It was there in all its glory, but after the address and phone number of Whitlock's new boat company, it read, *Coastal trips by paddle steamer. A new experience coming soon to Whitby. Luxury accommodation, hot meals, bar, flush toilets on board, seating for 52.*

I groaned because I had allowed the error to creep in at the last minute, although I must admit I felt my readers would enjoy that little *faux pas*.

The following week, I would resume my insurance work full-time in the glorious moorland and countryside of the

North Riding of Yorkshire. Perhaps I would also become the full-time editor of the *Micklesfield Magazine* as well. Only time would tell, and I was happy to wait and see what the future held.